Something NEW

A DARK AGE-GAP, STALK-HER, SECOND CHANCE, MAFIA ROMANCE

HANNAH RIO

Something New

A DARK AGE-GAP, STALK-HER, SECOND CHANCE, MAFIA ROMANCE

FAMILIA VECE
BOOK 3

HANNAH RIO

CHAPTER ONE
Tuomo

She giggles as I pull her into the space beneath the stairway in the hall of my father's mansion.

I push her up against the wall, staring down at her.

Nerissa is the most beautiful girl I've ever seen. She is young and I know my father would be furious if he caught me kissing the maid's daughter, but I can't help who I fall in love with. My heart is in control of that, and who am I to question my heart?

At twenty-nine, I've never felt this way about anyone in my life. Girls fall over me, because of who I am, but not Nerissa. Nerissa is different. And no girl has ever made me want to willingly defy my father and get into trouble.

She is mature for her age, and even though she is just seventeen, I believe we've found true love in each other.

I close the door behind us, and we are pressed together in the small space beneath the stairs.

She giggles again and I press my finger over her lips. "Shh." I whisper. "They'll hear you."

She pushes her lips together, sealing them shut, falling silent. She looks up at me and has my full attention. Beautiful, bright hazel eyes that catch the light and when the sunshine hits them just right, they turn to gold.

She takes a soft breath and her lips part.

I wrap my hand around her jaw, unable to control this urge I've had since the moment I laid eyes on her. She is my world. She is my everything.

I want her and I don't care where she comes from or who her mother is. I don't care that my father would disapprove. I only care about her.

She lifts her chin towards me, and I lower my lips - inches away from hers. I can smell strawberries and ice cream on her warm breath. We snuck it from the kitchen earlier and ate it in the back of the garden where no one would see us. We like to spend time amongst the orange trees, hidden from the watchful eyes of my father and my brothers.

We can never spend too much time together. We always need to be careful.

I meant to just walk her back to her room - but instead I pushed her into the closet beneath the stairs. I wanted to kiss her between the trees, but I didn't. I regret it and now I am going to make up for it. And now I can smell strawberries on her breath and feel the heat of her beautiful body against mine.

My heart is beating so fast as I lean closer to her.

Closer, until there is no space between us anymore and my lips press into hers.

Her soft, warm, divine mouth opens, and she returns the kiss without hesitation.

Her lips are inviting, plump, pink and beautiful. Her tongue dances across my mouth and my blood boils, wild images flashing through my mind.

She is mine, and she was always meant to be mine.

I am holding her so close, her heart beating so hard I can feel it - and mine is in sync with hers. It is the most beautiful moment I've ever experienced in my life.

That is - until the door flies open and someone grabs me by the arm - yanking me away from her and throwing me to the floor with vicious coldness.

I gasp in shock, staring up at my father.

"What the fuck do you think you are doing, *boy*?" he snarls at me, his mouth curled up with anger and disgust. "She is a child - a *maid's* child. *What the fuck do you think you are doing*? I asked you a question."

The veins on his head popping and blue. They do that when he's furious - and he's always angry.

"I love her." Is all I can say. "And don't call me boy. I stopped being a boy years ago." I snap. Although, when I am around my father, I always feel like a child. He knows how to make a person perceive themselves as small and worthless. He has never treated me like a man. He has never given me that respect or an ounce of love.

My twin brother, born mere minutes before me, is his pride and joy. Masaccio gets everything and I don't even get the left-over scraps. He looks at me *with a familiar* look of disgust. My father only has disdain towards me. He hates me and he never misses an opportunity to remind me of that.

I push myself up onto my knees as my father grabs Nerissa from the closet. She is crying, and she lifts her hands up to protect her face as he raises his hand as though he wants to slap her.

I am on my feet in a flash, grabbing his wrist. He is stronger than me. He always has been. A brute of a man, with an icy heart.

"Don't you dare hurt her." I scream in anger.

He releases her, turning to face me again. I would rather his attention be on me, anyway. Anything to keep her safe.

"If you didn't sneak around trying to take advantage of the *help*, you wouldn't put me in this position, and I wouldn't be forced to take action like this."

"I am not taking advantage of her." I snarl, clenching my fists at my side.

"He didn't take advantage of me, sir—" Nerissa says, full of fear and hesitation, but showing how much she loves me by standing up for me.

He spins towards hers with hate in his eyes. "Did I give you permission to speak, girl?"

She freezes, wide eyed like an animal in a trap.

"Don't speak to her like that." I say, pulling his attention back to me.

My father grabs the collar of my shirt and lifts me off the ground. My feet hang limp and useless in the air. I gasp for breath.

"Let me make this clear, you piece of shit. If I ever catch you near her again, I will cut off your balls and send her so far away from here, you will forget she ever existed. It will be your fault that her mother loses her job in this mansion. You will be the reason her life falls apart. I cannot afford for people to be talking about my son - *a Vece son* - running around with an underaged girl who is nothing but a *maid's* daughter."

My father drops me to the floor and grabs Nerissa's arm again. He drags her down the passage towards her mother's bedroom. They live in a small room together in the staff quarters. I am never supposed to be in that part of the house. And Nerissa is never supposed to leave the workers' side of the mansion. Of course, we've been sneaking around for months, visiting each other, spending time together. This was the first time I dared to kiss her - and it was everything I've dreamed of - but my father ruins all my dreams. He ruins everything. He is going to ruin my life if he takes her away from me.

I follow behind my father as he pushes Nerissa into her mother's room. I hear him screaming at her.

"I told you to keep your brat of a daughter on a leash. And tell her to cover up. What the fuck is she doing parading herself like that around my sons? My sons don't want trash like this. They deserve better and they are reserved for better than anything she could ever offer."

"Sir — I am so sorry — I didn't know — I told her —" Her mother stammers in fear. I can hear the stress in her voice. If she loses her job, she loses everything. Her home, her income, her security.

"I don't give a fuck about what you told her in the past. It didn't work. I am making it very clear now that if you don't pull her leash tighter, I'll remove you both permanently. I will make sure that you never work anywhere in this city again. Do I make myself clear?"

There is a moment of silence, and I can hear both Nerissa and her mother crying. My heart is breaking for Nerissa. She will blame herself. It's not her fault, it's mine. She doesn't deserve to be treated like this.

"I - I understand. It won't happen again. Ever." Her mother sniffles.

My father glares into the room for a moment longer, and then turns away.

His face is pulled into a sour scowl as if he's bitten into a lemon.

I hate him.

I hate him for doing this.

I hate him for embarrassing me.

I hate him for trying to keep me away from the first person I've ever loved.

He stalks towards me, his eyes locked onto mine. Predatory, he's like a lion moving in for the kill. I know what is coming — it's going to hurt.

Without hesitation, he grips me by the throat and body-slams me into the wall with enough force to move the painting hanging beside me.

"Did you hear everything?" he hisses into my face. "You like to eavesdrop." He yanks my ear. I think he might rip it off.

"Yes." I choke, my hatred growing deeper.

"Good. Then stay away from that little whore. You'll catch the clap sleeping with filth." He snarls. Then drops me. As I hit the floor, I clutch at my throat, choking for air.

I don't watch him walk away because I can't stand the sight of him.

I won't listen.

I won't ignore what I want any longer.

Nerissa belongs to me, and I always get what I want - no matter what I have to do. No matter who I have to step on. She is mine. She will always be mine.

CHAPTER TWO
Nerissa

It's late at night and luckily my mother is fast asleep when the small, folded piece of paper slips in through the open window of our bedroom. I grin, my heart fluttering with excitement. I climb out of bed, tip toeing across the wooden floors, avoiding the boards that squeak.

I peek out of the window, but Tuomo is nowhere to be seen outside. It's too dark. He's probably already run back around the front of the house, or up the back terrace stairs to avoid getting caught.

I pick up the secret note, tuck it into my shirt, and go back to bed.

I pull the blankets up over my body, making sure my mother doesn't stir. I wait to see if I have woken her. After a few minutes, when she's still snoring lightly, I unfold the note, squinting at his messy boy-handwriting. I only have the dim moonlight filtering through the window, making it hard to read the words.

Beautiful Nerissa, meet me behind the orange tree just before sunrise tomorrow. I can't wait to kiss you again. X

The butterflies in my stomach are fluttering so fast they could be mistaken for birds. Tuo is this thrill in my life, something exciting and forbidden, and so tempting.

He's a lot older than me and the thrill of having him chase me is like a drug. He is the first man I've ever kissed. I can't call him a boy. The guys at school are boys, Tuo is all man. I have a crush on him. It's dangerous and sexy, and I'm not going to deny it.

I shove the note under my pillow, closing my eyes tight as I try to fall asleep again, but I am too wound up.

He likes me. We kissed under the stairs, and my heart stopped and started just from the taste of his lips.

It's so thrilling, and dangerous, a forbidden love. We might even be a real-life Romeo and Juliette.

I was terrified when his father shouted at me earlier today, and I got so angry when he threatened my mother. I should know better than to challenge that old man. He's disgusting. She didn't deserve that. She works so hard every day. This job sucks the life out of her, but she still gets up and does it every day, so I can go to an excellent school and do better with my life. Her children have always come first.

I've got two older brothers, Jackson, and Blake, and both of them live here in the mansion, too. But they live a very different life than mine. Tuomo's father likes my brothers. They're useful, unlike me.

I guess, if I wanted his approval, I would've had to be a boy. To impress the old man, you need a penis, and to want to be a part of the sick, twisted mafia world he rules over. I don't have a dick, and I detest everything he stands for, so I will never be in his good graces.

I don't even want to be.

And I can't smile and be fake at parties like my brothers do. Rub shoulders with criminals and savages. Besides, I am not popular, or pretty, or strong, or athletic, or the life of *any* party. If I was, then the boys at school would chase me, like Tuo does.

I am nothing like my brothers. I love them dearly, but I'm not following in their footsteps. I don't want to be in the mafia or joining this sick and twisted family. I don't want my life to go down that slippery slope. I saw what Tuo's sister's life was like, what his brothers are like with women. This is fun, and forbidden, but I will not be a Vece.

I avoided Antonio Vece and all of his children pretty effectively until recently. All I ever used to do was focus on my schoolwork, sport and getting good grades. The things that can get me far away from here. But then Tuomo started playing this game, chasing me, distracting me with his charm and sex appeal. He's older than me. And I've never had such a good-looking man even glance in my direction, never mind chase me.

He's my first crush — it's a crush. A forbidden fling. That is fun and thrilling, but nothing more than that.

I take ages to fall asleep because I am so excited to meet Tuomo before sunrise. I dream of a knight in shining armor, a man of mystery and magic.

I wake up with a fright. For a second, I think I've overslept and missed the sunrise, but it's still dark. I slip out of bed and rush to the window. The sky is just lightening. I am just in time.

I pull off the giant tee shirt I sleep in and throw it onto the bed. Then I pull on my jeans and a black hoodie. The whole idea is not to be conspicuous, to seem like I'm just going to school early. I need to be unseen - it's a secret mission and I can't get caught.

I rush into the tiny bathroom my mother and I share and check my face, splashing water over my eyes to wake up. I brush my teeth, hoping the sound won't wake my mom.

When I am done, I sneak out of our room with my heart beating so hard against my ribs that it might break right through the bones.

The house is still silent. Most of the staff only start work at sunrise. The only ones who would be up now are the chefs, preparing breakfast and one cleaner to make sure everything is spotless before the master of the house gets up.

I tip toe down the passage to the back door that leads out past the washing lines. Only the staff ever come out here. I won't run into a lost Vece child here. I duck below the laundry that was hung up last night and creep along the side wall of the house towards the orange trees right at the back of the garden.

In spring, when all the citrus trees flower, it is one of my favorite smells in the entire world. All of those little white flowers smell like magic and freedom. It's sweet, intoxicating and beautiful.

It is late spring now, the blossoms have gone and the trees are just green with fresh shoots.

It's a little scary walking through the orchard in the dark. My shoulders are stiff, all my muscles tense.

"Tuomo?" I whisper, still trying to keep quiet.

Silence.

"Tuom—" he jumps out from behind a tree and locks his hand over my mouth. I scream, but thankfully he stops the sound from escaping.

His dark chuckle rumbles against my back as he pins me to his chest.

Tuomo leans close to my ear and whispers. "You should be careful. You don't know what could happen to such a beautiful creature, wondering out here all by herself in the dark."

His words send an erotic thrill through me. He runs his hand over my neck, down my chest, briefly caressing my breast. Then he steps away from me, and I'm dizzy with excitement from his touch.

He turns me to face him and even in the dim light of pre-dawn, he is gorgeous.

"Hello, little bird." He says, reaching out and twirling a loose curl of my hair in his finger.

"Hello." I grin.

"I'm sorry about what happened with my father. I hope you don't hate me for that."

I shake my head. "I could never hate you, Tuomo." With a bold sense of confidence surging through me, I take a step closer to him. "I do hate him, though."

I want to kiss him again. It was so magical last time.

His mischievous smile shows me he wants to kiss me, too. He wraps his hand around the back of my neck and pulls me hard against his solid, muscular body. He smells like sex on a stick - that cologne. I'd recognize it anywhere. Tuo smells like — Tuo. It's unique. He leans down and presses his lips into mine. He tastes even better than he smells, like sin and sugar.

I melt into him. The moment stops time. Nothing else exists. I'm more alive than I've ever been. In the cold, crisp air of dawn, I think I might be falling in love.

Tuomo leans away from me, then takes my hand in his.

"Little bird, do you know what you mean to me?" He asks, his voice serious.

I shake my head. Excited and nervous to hear his thoughts. What could I mean to him? Me - a little mousy girl with brown hair and sharp features. My lips are too full, and my eyes are way too big. I'm not pretty. I'm just average, with a bland face and a bland figure.

So, for Tuomo to be interested in me - it seems impossible. Too good to be real. Maybe this is a game he and his brothers are playing? It doesn't feel like a game when I'm with him.

I wait, focused only on him. What do I mean to him?

"You are my entire world. I've loved you from the moment I first saw you." His voice vibrates through me and his words carry me away as though they were being read aloud from a fairytale. Too farfetched to be true, but so tempting to believe.

"You - love me?" I stammer. "You don't love me, Tuo."

"I love you, and I don't care what my father - or anyone else says - I want you to be with me." He's lost his mind. Maybe he's drunk? The men in this house drink way too much. What am I supposed to say? I don't know what to do.

My lips part as I stare up at him. God, he's gorgeous. "I - I love you too, Tuomo." I say, unsure if I even know what love is yet, but it feels right to say it back to him.

"Let's make a promise to each other, little bird. A pact that can never be broken no matter how far apart we are - no matter what happens—"

His eyes are so dark right now, almost deadly serious. I nod again. Mesmerized by the way I, my whole body heats when he looks at me.

"What pact?"

"No matter where you are in the world - when you turn twenty-five years old - if you are not married or in love - then you will marry me."

It sounds like a fairy tale. Or a bad low budget Christmas movie. Either way, I know Tuomo Vece will never marry me. His father has a list of suitable brides for all his sons.

I giggle, loving the adventurous undertones of his pact. But he isn't laughing, and actually, he seems upset when I do.

I stop myself, clamping my mouth shut. He is older than me. He knows better than I do what love is. Maybe I will understand more when I turn twenty-five, and what harm can it do to say yes now? By the time I'm twenty-five, he'll be married and have forgotten about me.

"I promise." I say.

"You will marry me when you are twenty-five - no matter where you are?" He doesn't sound convinced.

"Yes." I grin, my heart fluttering at the daring prospect of marrying this man.

The smile that spreads across his face is worth every word I just said. Even if it was a lie.

I'm alight with the fire he ignites in me, but I can't shake the unsettling fear that I've just sold my soul to a devil.

Tuomo wraps his hand around my jaw and pulls me towards him to kiss me again.

I am young, falling in love, and filled with hope and romantic delusions. I allow him to sweep me away on a magic carpet ride of passion.

CHAPTER THREE
Tuomo

No. This can't be happening. I shake my head. My hands are shaking.

"What do you mean? Her mother is *dead*. How? What happened?" I snap, furious.

"They found her on the floor of the main bathroom. She was throwing up blood." Masaccio says, shrugging his shoulders. He doesn't care. He doesn't have a clue I am in love with the dead woman's daughter.

"People don't just throw up blood for no reason. What the fuck happened to her? Did someone do something to her?" My jaw drops open. "Did someone poison her?"

My eyes immediately go to my father, who is standing there, stoic, cold, with zero expression on his face.

I run at him, my fists clenched, ready to beat the truth out of him - but Rufino grabs me and holds me back. "Did you poison her mother?" I scream at my father.

My father brushes imaginary dust off his sleeve and looks at me as though I mean nothing. "Don't be so dramatic, Tuomo. What reason could I have to poison the housekeeper? She was probably sick. These people don't look after themselves." These people, he thinks they are less human than he is. His blood is just as red as hers. The only difference is he has the money to look after himself while he kept her so poor she couldn't.

Masaccio, my twin brother, pushes me back and stands between my father and me. "What has gotten into you, Tuomo? Why the hell do you care so much about the housekeeper?" He's confused. I'm angry over a situation that on any other day I wouldn't even notice.

"Don't you know - he's been fucking her daughter." Rufino chuckles. "His little plaything, they have been sneaking around fucking in broom closets. Now, with her mother dead, I suppose she won't be around here anymore."

My blood boils hotter, faster, angrier.

My fists are clenched so tight that my shoulders ache. I narrow my eyes at my father. "Are you going to send Nerissa away?" I ask, my heart already knowing the answer, but my mind refusing to accept the truth. He won't keep her here. This is what he wanted all along, a reason to get rid of her.

"Of course, I am. Why would she stay here? Her mother is dead. I don't employ her, she's a schoolgirl. There's no free lodging here."

"But Nerissa's brother's - they are still staying here, right?" I snarl. Those two assholes wouldn't take on the responsibility of caring for her, but I'll care for her. I just need her to stay.

"Well, they do work for me. So, yes." Then she can stay.

I want to kill him.

I want to kill my father so badly that I'm envisioning it, like a waking dream. I don't understand how he can do this to me. Why? Why would he take away the one thing that I have ever loved in this world?

Because he can. That's why.

I have to change his mind.

But right now, I am so angry that all I see is red, irrational rage, fueled by hatred. My world is spinning in and out of focus and I can't get my thoughts in line. If I stay here, I'll kill him.

I spin around and march out of the living room. I need to get away from all of them. My fucking brothers are cowards. They don't have the balls to stand up to him.

As soon as I leave, I hear the cackle of laughter.

It is funny for them.

This is amusing.

My pain entertains them.

My hatred is like venom. It's inside me, and when I do eventually get so angry I let it out, it will be deadly..

I walk right out of the house, into the garden. I don't stop walking. The property is massive enough

I can keep going. Big enough to walk off this rage. The excruciating pain that is radiating through my body, from my broken heart.

I stop when I reach the orange trees. I grab a branch to steady myself. The world has tilted on its axis and I'm falling off.

Hanging my head down, I try to even my breathing. But I can't. I am panicked. Fearful. Terrified.

He can't send Nerissa away. I'll die without her. She's what keeps me alive.

I would kill for her. I would do anything for her. I am in love with her.

Can't he see that? He sees — which is exactly why he will do it. To punish me, to remind me I'm second best.

He can't send her away.

Over the next few days, as my father prepares to take care of Nerissa - I become convinced that he killed her mother. He took her mother's life so that he would have a reason to send

Nerissa away, to punish me for falling in love. To prove a point.

He is watching Nerissa like a hawk, so I haven't been able to see her, or talk to her. He says that he has her under guard to make sure she doesn't steal anything before she leaves, but it's to keep me away. To make sure I feel the wrath of his punishment.

I haven't had a chance to comfort her or tell her how much I love her.

I want to tell her I am going to fight for her.

I beg and plead and promise my soul to him - but my father won't budge. He won't change his mind. Nothing I do now can keep her here, and even if she stayed, she has his attention. Her life would be hell.

He has arranged for Nerissa to live with another family, on the other side of the city, where she can no longer 'be a distraction for me'. At least he hasn't left her destitute on the streets, but her brothers would have asked questions if he did.

She is leaving in two days. I wanted to see her, to spend these precious few days together, but it has been impossible.

We are all sitting around the dinner table. My entire family. My brothers, my sister Dalila, and my father. Usually, dinner is filled with talk of business, or Dalila trying to convince my father to let her start horse riding or get a new car. He usually caves and gives her whatever her heart desires. She is spoiled.

Tonight, there is a hushed silence at the table, and everyone seems to glance at me when he's not looking.

They are waiting.

And I sit here knowing it is the wrong time and the wrong place - but I ask my father again.

"Why can't she stay, Dad? Why can't she live in her mother's room? She will be eighteen in a few months, and she can take over her mother's job." My desperation is humiliating, but I would do anything to keep her here.

My father has reached his last ounce of patience. He stands up, slamming his fists against the table and sending dishes rattling across it. My sister's glass of water topples over, making a mess across her plate of food.

But she doesn't say a word. No one says a word. We all know never to speak when my father is like this, or we will become the focus of his anger. But tonight, I am desperate. I don't care how angry he is. I'm dying inside and I will not stop until there is no hope left.

"What the fuck is wrong with you, boy?" He screams at me.

"I love her." I scream back. "Do you have any idea what love is? Have you ever loved anything besides yourself?"

My father reaches across the table and grabs me by the collar. With his other hand, he slams his fist into my face. The metal of his signet ring brands my cheek, and his knuckles crunch against my cheekbone.

I'm falling. I want to hit him back, to fucking fight him for her, but I'm not strong enough.

Next thing I am waking up on the dining room floor with my brothers and my sister standing over me.

"Dude, what the fuck is wrong with you? Have you lost your gad damned mind challenging him like that? He will kill you," Celso says, holding out his hand to help me up.

I push it away. Embarrassed, and in pain, my eye is throbbing. I can barely open it.

Celso huffs and walks away. Rufino grabs my hand and drags me to my feet.

"Get your shit together, idiot. You are making a fool of yourself over a girl. If you carry on like this, he will end up killing her, too." He laughs as though it's a joke, but in his eyes, there is a streak of seriousness. He also believes my father killed her mother.

My stomach rolls as a wave of nausea washes over me.

I don't know what else to do.

It's useless. I can't win against him. I have no control over my life.

I shove past my siblings and leave the dining room on shaky legs. My head is pounding, and I need an ice-pack and an advil. But most importantly, I need to speak to Nerissa.

I walk straight to the staff's side of the house, straight to her room.

I shove the door open without knocking. "Nerissa," I say, walking in.

But it's empty.

Not just empty - I mean barr*en*.

There is no bed, no cupboard, no clothing, no curtains.

Nothing.

She is gone. Every trace of her erased, like she never existed.

She is already gone.

My father has sent her away, and I didn't even get the chance to say goodbye.

I fall to my knees, clutching my aching chest and fighting tears of anguish.

"Tuomo?" Her voice comes from behind me, and I jump to my feet and spin around.

"I thought you were gone." I stammer, rushing to her and dragging her into my arms.

"They had to deep clean this room. I was staying in the room across the hall. They said my mother might have contaminated it." She bursts into tears so full of pain that they rip through her body, making her shudder in my arms.

I hold her tighter.

"They are sending me away." She whispers between heavy breaths.

"I heard. I don't want you to go."

"I'm scared. I don't even know where I'm going. I miss my mom—"

I thread my fingers through her hair along the back of her head and hold her face against my chest.

"I will find you, little bird. Wherever they take you, I will find you. I promise you. Remember our pact. Ok. No matter what happens, just remember the pact."

She nods against my chest, her tears soaking through my shirt and her whimpering cries muffled against me.

"Will you remember the pact, little bird?"

"I will." She whispers, leaning away from me. "I will remember it."

"Good." I say, brushing a strand of hair from her face. "I love you."

She sniffs. "I - I love you." She says, speaking softly, distracted, lost.

She must be heartbroken that she is being taken away from me. She must be as heartbroken as I am. But I will find her again. I made a promise to her, and I will keep it. She belongs with me. She always has and she always will.

I dip my hand into my pocket, remembering the gift I have for her.

I pull out a small plastic charm. A toy from a chocolate packet. It made me smile because it made me think of her. I push it into her palm and close her fingers around it. "Next time we meet, I will give you a diamond." I say.

She looks down at her hand, at the little plastic bird. She smiles.

"Thank you, Tuomo."

CHAPTER FOUR
Nerissa

I found my mother in a pool of her own blood, it is an image I don't think I will ever forget. There are things you can't erase from your mind, the horror of that sight is one of them.

Every time I close my eyes, I see it.

And every time it makes me cry, and the same surge of panic and pain pulse through me.

I remember falling to my knees at her side, rolling her over and seeing the blood smeared across her mouth, and her eyes - they were white, frosted over, lifeless and empty.

I screamed her name. I screamed until all I was doing was screaming.

People rushed in and pulled me away from her.

I fought to get back to her side, but they shoved me into another room and one of the other housekeepers made me shower.

I was shaking, my entire body convulsing, and I couldn't make it stop.

They asked me questions I didn't hear or understand. All I could see was my mother drowning in her own blood.

Finally, a doctor injected something into my arm and the entire world went black.

When I woke up the next morning though, my head thick and heavy, the first thing I remembered was my mother and I broke down again. The staff scolded me and said I should shut-up. I'd cause trouble making a scene.

I knew she was dead and that I would never see her again, my world fell apart. How I am supposed to carry on like this?

I don't know how I am supposed to live with this pain inside me.

That day, and every day since then, I've cried. Lost, broken and in denial.

Every time I sleep, which is often because all I want to do is escape reality, I wake up and remember it all over again. I want to die too. I can't think of anything or anyone else. I can barely breathe, never mind eating, drinking, or bathing.

I do want to die. I want to be with my mother.

I have lost the most special person in the world. The only person who was there for me. The only person who loved me.

When the lady who manages all the staff comes to talk to me late in the afternoon, I can't focus.

"Nerissa, honey, I need you to listen."

I nod. She is sitting on the end of the single bed where I have been lying all day. Unable to move. Not able to function.

"Honey, the boss has arranged for you to go and stay somewhere new. It's closer to your school. You will be taken care of there."

My mind registers some of what she is telling me. "I am not staying here? My brothers are here."

"Yes, honey. They think it is better if you aren't in this house anymore. After what happened."

"Why?" I ask, terrified of the idea of leaving the last place I saw my mother. The only place that reminds me of her. Terrified of leaving her behind.

"I don't know honey, but it's what the boss wants. He had a meeting with your brothers, and they have decided." She puts a hand on my back to try comfort me. "Remember, it will be closer to your school, and you love school. You can focus on that. It will be good for you."

I nod, I can't even imagine studying ever again. I only have a year of high school left. I wanted to go to university. My grades are good enough to get a scholarship - but right now - it all seems pointless. I did that for my mom, to make her proud. Everything is for nothing without her.

But regardless of what I want, or think - the plans are in motion, and I just sit back and watch them as they pack my things into suitcases and prepare for me to be moved somewhere unknown. My brothers haven't even bothered to come see me, even though they are in this house. They could decide to send me away, but they can't look me in the eye and tell me themselves.

I'm scared, and numb.

My brothers are all staying here. And I don't think it's fair - but no one cares what I think. My mother is dead. My mother. She is gone. My heart will never heal from this. My life will never be the same. I will never be ok again.

All I can do is cry.

And it is all I do. I sit quietly, in the room opposite where I used to stay with my mother, and I cry. Day after day while they prepare to send me away.

I cry.

The other staff avoid me, or pretend they can't hear me.

One evening I am sitting on the bed staring at the door, across the hall, to my mother's room.

I don't know how long I've been sitting there, but Tuomo appears, shoving my mother's bedroom door open and storming inside. My heart aches I want him to close it. I haven't looked inside since she died. The door has been closed.

Tuomo says my name.

I blink. Trying to process what is happening. He says my name again and then collapses to the floor.

I get up and walk across the hall, I haven't seen him in days. I haven't even thought about him to be honest. I haven't thought about anything except my mother. Why is he here?

"Tuomo?" I whisper, and when he spins around and comes towards me, I tense up.

"I thought you were gone." He says, dragging my stiff body into his arms.

"They had to deep clean this room. I was staying in the room across the hall." Telling the story makes my throat tighten and my words become too much to handle. A lump forms in my throat and again tears spill down my cheeks.

He holds me so tight that it hurts. But I like the pain. I like the constriction of being locked in his harms. "They are sending me away." I tell him.

"I heard. I don't want you to go."

"I'm scared. I don't even know where I'm going. I miss my mom—"

He strokes my head, and I wish he was rather holding me tight again. I want the pain instead.

"I will find you, little bird. Wherever they take you, I will find you. I promise you. Remember our pact. Ok. No matter what happens just remember the pact."

He was talking, I wasn't paying attention. I nod, because I don't know what he said.

"Will you remember the pact, little bird?"

Oh. The pact. How can he think about that now? "I will." I say, wondering if he cares about what happened to my mother. "I will remember it."

"Good." He touches my face. "I love you."

His words are nothing to me, empty noise. I am so numb. "I - I love you." I can't deal with him right now. I'm going to cry again. I want to scream and claw at my chest because the pain is unbearable. I want to run and jump off a cliff and fall to my death so that I can be with my mom.

I know I don't want to die.

But I wish I could stop hurting so much.

I wish I could have her back.

Tuomo takes my hand and opens my fingers. He puts something into my hand and then closes my fingers around it. "Next time I see you, I will give you a diamond." He says.

I look down at my hand and the small plastic toy inside it.

A bird.

A little plastic bird.

Because he calls me little bird.

I sigh, not sure what to say. His gift doesn't break through the numbness, it's just a bird in my hand.

"Thank you, Tuomo."

♥

That was the last time I saw Tuomo, the next morning before the sun came up, they gathered my things and loaded me into a car. All of my belongings in a few bags. My life reduced to almost nothing at all.

I didn't even care, when they drove me away from that house.

I was numb. Numb to everything. I had been hurting so much that I didn't have enough energy in me to be afraid of where they were sending me.

I just wanted to get there and think about something else. Anything else.

You will be closer to your school.

I sigh as they drive me towards the other side of the city away from their wealthy neighborhood, to my new life.

I guess I will do what I have always done, focus on my studies. Ignore the world around me, get good grades and be the best that I can be. I will do anything and everything I can to make sure that I become someone my mother would be proud of. This is a chance to be more, to make her dreams for me come true, and I need to make the most of it.

It only takes thirty minutes to get to the house I will stay in. Thirty minutes, but my old life feels so far away, like is it on another planet.

Everything and everyone in the Vece mansion disappears from my thoughts as I walk up the steps into my new home.

I will be cleaning here, and going to school, and studying. That is all I need to focus on.

Everything is going to be ok, Nerissa. I tell myself.

I do my best not to cry during the day when there are people around me, but for months I cry myself to sleep. It is only after I graduate high school, I start to feel like myself. I find my feet again.

Instead of crying at night I talk to my mom. I tell her about my day and what I learned and who I met and that I have new friends.

Slowly, the pain starts to ease and even though I miss her, I focus on other things.

When I am granted a scholarship to a local university, I'm overjoyed, my life isn't over. I still have something beautiful waiting for me in my future.

CHAPTER FIVE
Tuomo

It's been almost six years since I spoke to Nerissa.

But I see her every day.

I follow.

I watch.

I wait.

We are meant to be together, so as soon as she turns twenty-five, I intend to keep my promise to marry her.

Over the years Nerissa has become more and more beautiful. She was always beautiful. The most beautiful girl in the world. Her thick dark brown hair, those gorgeous, big green eyes and her plump peach-colored lips - she has always been perfect.

But now she has filled out in different ways. She has grown from a girl into a woman. Her curves are more accentuated, and her features are more defined.

She is striking.

Mesmerizing.

I sit in the car outside her university. She has already graduated but today she came to fetch the last of her books from her locker. She has them in her arms as she walks, unknowingly, towards where I am parked. My windows are too dark for her to see into my car though. She has walked past me many times. The boy she likes is walking across the grass with her and I watch them, my fist clenched on the steering wheel.

He is getting too close. Too comfortable around *my* girl.

I waited, hoping she would lose interest in him once university was over, but this one she seems to really like and the last boy she really liked kissed her before I managed to - *intervene*.

Nerissa doesn't know I follow her. She is blissfully unaware I play any part in her life at all. So, she also does not know that the last boy who liked her didn't change to another university like the rumors stated. He was purposefully removed from the picture.

Because no one else should dare to kiss her. And no one else should dare to touch her.

And right now, I am watching as the boy reaches out and puts his hand on her lower back. His name is Riley. And Riley doesn't know that soon he is also going to mysteriously disappear.

She turns to look at him with a smile on her face and a bright light shining in her eyes.

I snarl, my eyes darkening towards him.

I wish I could climb out of the car right now and slam my fists into his face until his nose splinters and his teeth crack.

But I can't. I have to be patient.

Her birthday is coming up. In a week she turns twenty-five and as long as there is no boy she is in love with - and she is not married - then our pact will stand strong. Nerissa will have to keep the promise she made almost six years ago and marry me.

So, all I have to do is make sure that this boy doesn't make it to her birthday.

Even though my father moved her out of the house, I could never let go of her. I have watched her throughout her life as she grew and changed and become more and more enticing to me.

I know all her favorite foods and her favorite color. I remember which sweater she loves the most, even though it has holes at the seams, she refuses to throw it out. And in the evenings, she curls up on the sofa to watch tv wearing that same black hoodie.

She loves popcorn, but without salt. She throws chili flakes on it.

She loves coffee with one spoon of sugar and way too much milk.

She loves it when it rains, and I watch her staring through the window, looking up at the dark gray sky with a smile on her face.

Sometimes at night, lying in bed right before she falls asleep, she talks to her mother.

Sometimes she doesn't.

And some nights - she touches herself - and those nights are the most difficult for me, especially when I am in her room, standing in the dark, watching her from my hiding place behind her closet. Those nights are hard for me because all I want to do is be with her. I want to walk over to her bed and give her what she needs.

But I have to stay dead still, my cock rock hard against my pants, my breathing steady and silent while I watch her. That is self-control.

The self-control I have shown for six years, waiting for her to turn twenty-five, is something that most people couldn't do.

It is true love.

Nerissa walks past my car and I hear part of their conversation.

"So, you are coming to my birthday, right?"

"Of course." He laughs. "I wouldn't miss it. And I have something really special to tell you - at your party, you have to wait."

"Why can't you tell me now?" She giggles.

"No, it's - its special. I'll wait for the right time." He grins.

In my mind I picture the horrendous things I am going to do to him. I picture the terror in his eyes and how he will beg. They always beg, as though it will help them.

The images in my mind help to stop me from getting out my car and killing him right now.

In the rear-view mirror, I watch Nerissa hug him goodbye. Then she climbs into her beat-up little hatchback and I follow her to the mall. I know she came here today to get a dress for her birthday. She has been talking to her friends about it for weeks. I know which one she wants because she keeps looking at it in the window, but it's not the one she can afford.

I've bought it for her, and when she goes to stare into the window today, it won't be there anymore.

Because it is going to be delivered to her apartment after she gets home this evening - from an anonymous friend wishing her an amazing birthday.

There have been so many times when I've wanted to confront her and tell her I still love her. To expose myself and show her how much I care. I've wanted to - but I haven't because I will honor the pact that we made. I will wait until she turns twenty-five in six short days.

A t the mall Nerissa walks around, taking her time to go from store to store to find an affordable dress she can wear to her birthday party. None of them are 'the' dress, and she isn't excited when she tries them on. I enjoy watching her try on the different styles, lengths, and designs - but I know that the one I got her is the dress that will not only make her body look like sin, but it will light up those fucking gorgeous eyes.

When she gets to the shop where the dress, she loves was in the window her face falls. She reaches up and touches the glass where her dress used to be.

Nerissa's smile fades she sighs, then shrugs ever so slightly and walks away. I grin, watching her from a distance.

I can't wait for her to see that dress, when the elegant gift box arrives, and she opens it. Her face will be priceless, worth every cent I paid for the dress.

After a while Nerissa chooses a short, pale pink tight fighting dress. It's covered in glittering patterns and hugs her body just right.

She looks incredible. I will have to take her out on a date so that she can wear this one - but on her birthday I know she will wear the other dress.

After shopping she buys herself a coffee to-go and strolls back to her car.

I follow her through the afternoon traffic to her apartment and park in my spot, from here I can see inside her window on the second floor.

The dress is waiting for her at the front desk, through the glass doors I watch the security guard duck behind the counter and hand her the package.

She looks shocked, then examines the box which does not have any details on it, no name and no return address.

I wait until I see her in the window of her apartment.

She places the box on the table and opens it.

I feel a sense of excitement run through me. I wish she knew it was from me. Maybe she does. Maybe she has been waiting to turn twenty-five - waiting for me.

Nerissa pulls the lid off the box and gasps. Her hand is over her mouth as she stares down into the box and from here it looks like she might even be crying.

She brushes her fingers across her cheeks, then wipes her hands on her jeans before lifting the dress out of the box.

Fuck. It's going to be incredible on her.

Pitch black, sequined, tight and short. The thin shoulder straps will show off those gorgeous collar-bones of hers and her long neck - dipping into that full cleavage she often tries to hide.

She lifts the box, searching inside, looking for a card, or a note. But there isn't one.

Nerissa picks up her phone and dials her friend.

I switch my phone to the app that tracks her calls so that I can listen in.

"Hayley, did you do this?" She asks with laughter in her voice.

"Sorry, what? Um - you are going to have to be more specific, Nissa. I do a lot of things."

"The dress?"

"Still not following." Her friend isn't responsible for the gift.

"The one that I showed you in the window last week - you are the only one who I showed - and I just got home, and it was waiting for me at reception."

"Someone bought you that dress and delivered it to your apartment?"

"Yes. that is what I just said."

"Girl, it wasn't me - you must have told someone else."

"No, I only told you—" Nerissa didn't tell anyone else.

"Dammit - I have to run - I'll call later ok - Just try remember who else you told." There's a ruckus in the background and the call ends abruptly.

Nerissa stares from her phone to the dress, confused.

I love that I'm the one who made her eyes shine, and gave her the smile that still hasn't faded away.

CHAPTER SIX
Nerissa

I stare at the box on the table, running back and forth through my memory to figure out who might have been with me when I commented on the dress. But the harder I think the less I come up with. For the life of me the only person I can remember being around and talking to about the dress is Hayley.

I have a lot of friends, but most of them are just friends at university we don't hang out or go shopping together. They are casual acquaintances I met through my classes. Hayley is my closest friend, the type of friend who would pull off a surprise like this - well - that is - if she could afford it. But she really can't.

We are all students working shitty jobs just to get by.

I pull my mouth to the side. Hayley says she didn't do it, and it would have taken her a half a year to save up for a dress like this - so it definitely wasn't her. Even if she had the money, she would never be stupid enough to spend an amount like that on one dress. It would be careless. She is more levelheaded and sensible than that.

But who then?

Riley? Could it have been him?

No, he's amazing, but he's not romantic like this - I mean - what do I know though? Maybe he is. It's not like we are dating yet. We might be, after he talks to me at my birthday, and we become an official couple, I will find out he is romantic. He could have done this for me as some kind of pre-gesture, to make sure I say yes when he asks me out. I was going to say yes, anyway. I like him so much.

I giggle and spin with the dress pressed up against my body.

It is gorgeous. I've been in love with it since I first laid eyes on it. It became this mystical unicorn. The dress I could never have. The girl I want to be could afford this dress, but not me. It was unattainable and a reminder of my position in life. I'm average, just a student trying to get through my degree so I can afford to buy a dress like this one day.

It's strange how much power we can put into a lifeless, useless object. It's crazy how it can represent something completely different from what it is. A status. A lifestyle. A person. A dream.

"Well, you have graduated now, and you start your new job in just over a month - so technically, you can be *anyone* and *anything* you want to be. You can be the girl who wears this dress. You can be amazing." I tell myself, standing in front of the tall mirror next to my bed in my bachelor apartment.

It's small and cramped in here, but its home sweet home to me.

I have set up the space with pictures on the walls, fairy lights hanging from corner to corner and big textured pillow on my blue, purple and pink comforter.

No one else comes in here but me anyway - and Hayley. We sometimes drink wine on a Wednesday and discuss the horrible chapters we had to study that week. It's so crazy to think that university is over now. Our Wednesday night wine evenings are going to be us talking about work and the people or clients who annoy us. We're actual adults, that is scary.

My other friends don't know me like Hayley knows me.

They all think I am a bit bland. I am, I wear neutral colors and always having my hair tied up. I almost never put make-up on.

But I don't have the right to dress up like the gorgeous girls do. Because I am not gorgeous, or special, or anything but me. It's just not who I am.

I'm not beautiful - not by the fashion magazine standards. My eyes are still way too big. My lips are puffy like am pouting without even trying. At least my body has filled out as I got older, not so gangly and skinny. God gave me a few curves, but not any idea what to do with them. I blame not having my mom around anymore, there was no one to show me how to go from girl to woman.

I get nervous when boys kiss me. So, I just avoid it. I don't really date because every guy I fall for seems to just ghost me. And it hurts. *Every single time* it hurts. The number one personality trait guys in university possess is, asshole. They are all assholes.

I can't believe I am going to be twenty-five in a few days.

It's crazy how the time has flown. Just the other day I was - wow - I kissed that Vece boy. Tuomo. Oh, my word. I'm turning twenty-five.

I giggle, remembering the silly, childish pact we made we would get married. Wow, that really was another life. I haven't thought about him since the day I left. After my mother died I blocked out the Vece mansion and all the pain it held.

My heart pangs when I think about her.

I was going through so much then. I didn't have time to think about the people I left there. Tuomo was this guy who chased me, he made my heart race, and it was devious and forbidden.

All I remember now is how incredibly hot he was.

He was the older boy, a forbidden fantasy.

But now I am a lot wiser. I understand the truth about that Vece family and who they truly are. Who Tuomo is. I want nothing to do with them.

I want nothing to do with the mafia.

My brothers are still tied up in that mess and it is not a good life. I can see the struggles they go through. Antonio Vece uses them. He doesn't care about anyone.

People that rich - all they care about is money and power - not other people.

I am lucky I got out of there when I did. I am lucky I got away from all of them. Especially Tuomo. He's probably just like his father.

Although, I remember how hot kissing him was.

I laugh as I walk through my tiny bathroom and turn on the shower.

I want to get ready for bed, then I can grab my laptop and start following up with whoever hasn't RSVP'd for my birthday party. I have saved up for a month to have an amazing night and I want everyone there.

My bathroom fills up with steam. I glance at the window, thinking I should close the blinds, but it's already so steamed up I can't even see out of it, so I don't bother. No one can see in.

I step under the hot flow of water and as it splashes over me, I think about how far I've come. It's been forever since I thought about the Vece mansion.

Losing my mother was more pain than I would wish on my worst enemy. But it was the catalyst I needed to get out of that life and start a new one. I had no choice. They didn't want me — them sending me away saved me.

And once I was out, I had support of the people I lived with until I moved into this tiny apartment, and started making a better life for myself.

I learned how to be independent, how to be responsible with money, how to take care of myself and save at the same time. Leaving there forced me to grow up.

I am going to do big things. I've got massive goals, big dreams, and plans to reach each one.

Graduating in the top five of my year, I was offered a job before I even finished university. Head hunted by a very prestigious law firm. I start in a month. It's a low-down position, clerical work. But it's a foot in the door and a chance to be seen and make a name for myself. There's potential for me to work my way up, and hard work doesn't scare me.

I'm over the moon excited about it.

I get out of the shower and sigh in annoyance. I left my towel hanging over the back of my bed again.

I run, dripping, through the tiny apartment and grab it, wrapping the fluffy warmth around my body before I wet the entire floor.

I grab a smaller towel for my hair because it's so long and thick and takes forever to dry, so it needs its own towel.

I grin again when I see the dress on the table. I can't believe someone bought it for me. It must have been Riley. He's great, I think he might be the one.

I might lose my virginity to him. Not that I have told him I'm a virgin, God. I just said I wanted to take things slow.

He seems like the perfect guy - sweet, polite, caring and gentle. He's got a good job, and a plan for his life. When I talk he listens, he respects me. Also, he hasn't ghosted me.

Still wrapped in the towel I grab my laptop and flop down onto my bed.

I email the venue where I am hosting my birthday - a club in the middle of town - a popular place I have never been to. I confirm the table I have reserved in the VIP section. Then I go through the list of people I have invited and message those who haven't replied. People can be so rude about these things.

Most of my friends are going to be there. In fact, I think a lot of people I didn't even invite are going to be there. In university if one person hears about a party it is assumed that everyone is invited. Especially in a club.

Partying is not my style - I look up at the black dress, glittering near the window - a new me. Time to reinvent myself. For one night I *can be* the pretty girl. The dress could be like Cinderella and magically make me confident and beautiful.

Well - I can wish.

When I am done on my laptop, I throw the towels over the back of my bed again, and pull on my sweatpants and a crop top. I braid my damp hair because I really don't have the energy to dry it now.

I lift my blankets and climb into bed, snuggling into the warmth.

I fall asleep with a smile on my face, thinking about Riley seeing me in the dress he bought me - and wondering what shoes I should wear with it. I'll ask Hayley. She's a fashion queen. She'll help me pull the whole outfit together.

CHAPTER SEVEN
Tuomo

It's done. I roll my shoulders back trying to force the tension out of them.

I dust my hands down the sides of my pants, rubbing the dirt and soil off them. I hate the stickiness of blood, it's fucking disgusting. Washing it off takes ages, and it gets everywhere. But I had to do, what I had to do.

I bend down to grab the shovel off the ground and toss it into the open trunk of my car.

It's dark, and it's a long ass drive to get back to the city. I should hurry. I came here and did what I had to do, dawdling isn't part of the plan.

It's done and that asshole won't be showing up at her birthday party to tell her anything special.

No secret, special message for the girl who doesn't belong to him. He was becoming a problem, him and his being a perfect ten.

He won't show up anywhere ever again.

I didn't intend to get rid of him tonight. I planned to sort this minor problem out a few days ago, but then the boy changed his plans, and I had to switch a few things around. It doesn't matter. As long as it was sorted before her birthday party, I couldn't have him showing up putting ideas in her head. I would do anything for her, always. I will change my entire schedule and flip my world upside down it if means I get her.

I glance at my watch and see that I have just enough time to get back home, shower, and change before I need to be at the club for Nerissa's party. I didn't get an invitation, but I'd already invited myself.

A surge of energy pulses through me, a zap, like lighting spiking through a pitch black, midnight sky.

I have waited so long for this night. It's surreal that it is finally here. I have thought about it every day for six years. I have fantasized and imagined how it would go. And now it's here. Tonight. It's happening.

Slamming the trunk closed I climb into the driver's seat. I have booked the car for a valet tomorrow. Just to be safe. Most of the law is in my father's pocket, but I prefer not to take the risk, anyway. Perfect ten, rich boy might have a daddy that goes all nuts about him being missing.

Tonight, I will take another car to the club.

The drive home takes forever, not really, it's the same distance it always is, but I am anxious. I want this to be perfect and I have so much anticipation building inside me. So much tension. It's exhilarating, but I'm nervous.

I am going to ask her to marry me.

After waiting years, being patient and biding my time - I am about to ask the girl of my dreams to marry me. The only girl who is and will ever be meant for me.

I will ask her, she will say yes, and that is when my life becomes perfect.

No more waiting and watching from the sidelines, no more patience needed. No more self-control when other men make moves on her.

At home I shower in a hurry. I want to be there the moment she arrives.

I want to see her in that dress.

I wear my custom-made black tuxedo. A crisp black shirt and my black belt.

She will be impressed when she sees me, she's not the only one that has grown up.

As soon as she sets eyes on me, she will remember that we are meant to be together.

She has probably been waiting for this day with as much eagerness as I have.

I take the Maserati. Matte black.

It growls as I race through to the city towards the club.

I don't really need to hide from her anymore. I don't need to fade into the background, but I am still going to do so. If she notices me tonight -

that will be fine.

But my plan isn't to talk to her in this noisy, polluted, crowded place.

I am going to wait until afterwards, when we can be alone, in peace and privacy. I want her to myself, not like this with everyone around.

It is going to be intimate.

The most perfect moment of my life.

I park right outside the club and walk straight past the waiting line of people.

They know me here. They know me at every club in this city. Not because I go clubbing often - but because of who I am. Vece Holdings owns almost every night time entertainment venue in the city, we do not wait in lines.

Everyone knows the Vece family, and everyone has enough respect to stay out of our way.

The club is already packed with drunk and high assholes, jumping around on the dance floor. Nerissa has booked the VIP table upstairs overlooking the main dance floor, so I head to the bar and make sure I am in a position where I can see that part of the club. Later on, I will make my way upstairs. For now, I am fine right over here.

I order a whisky on the rocks and sip it.

There is a loud commotion at the door which I can hear even over the pumping bass of the club speakers. Someone screams *happy birthday* and then a bunch of girls shout excitedly.

Nerissa has just walked in, and her friends are already dragging her towards the bar, yelling 'shots'.

She is smiling from ear to ear and she - looks - fucking - incredible.

That dress - fuck. Wow. So worth it.

I take a deep breath as my body stirs to life. She always has this effect on me, but dressed like that, it's doubled. She never dresses up. She prefers comfort over fashion. And I love that about her. But, seeing her like this is a rare treat that every inch of my mind and body is loving.

A dark smile spreads across my lips as I watch her take a shot of tequila and pull a sour face.

I guess she is the reason I don't go partying and clubbing much. Unless it is business related.

Because when I am not working or attending to family business, I am watching her.

So, whatever she likes to do - is what I like to do.

The night rolls on and I am watching her from a corner table I reserved in VIP section. Strangers come past and sit at the table with me, some make out with each other, some are too drunk to care that they are being rude. I don't chase them away. Having other people around me makes me less obvious.

I don't even care they are there.

All I care about his her.

My eyes are on her.

She has so many friends around her. They are all laughing and joking and having a blast.

I feel a pang of jealously because it is the type of life I have always been curious about.

My life is nothing like this.

I have control, rules, structures, a family I have to obey, a father who is monstrously demanding of my time and energy while giving me nothing in return. Nothing but trauma and misery.

I hate him for sending Nerissa away all those years ago. I hate him for denying me the love of my life.

I hate him because he adores Masaccio and even though Mas is my twin - it is made clear to me daily that I cannot compare to him. I am nothing compared to my twin - and it's all because he was born a mere few minutes before I was.

The first-born son - and the runt. That is how my father views it.

Nerissa leans close to a friend as they converse over the music.

She has the eyes of every man in this place on her - and she looks like a goddess - but I can see something else in her eyes.

Sadness. Disappointment.

"I haven't heard from him today." Her friend says, shaking her head.

"He promised he would be here." Nerissa says, looking around with her brows knotted together.

Riley.

That fucking boy.

Well, princess, he won't be here. He will never be part of your life ever again. I made sure of that.

It annoys me she is so upset by his absence.

But I push it aside because after tonight it won't matter.

Nothing else but her and I will matter.

Our worlds will converge, and we can be together as we were always meant to be.

Nerissa accepts that Riley is not going to show up, and she focuses on her friends and the party. She has an incredible night and near the end, when I can see she is getting ready to leave, I stand up to leave as well.

I want to get there before her.

I want to surprise her.

My excitement blooms like a wildfire on an open, dry field.

"Soon, little bird." I smile, taking one last look at her gorgeous figure and that beautiful face - then I leave the VIP section. Disappearing into the crowded space below as I push my way to the exit.

I climb into my car, a smile etched onto my face.

I open the glove box and pull out the small velvet box inside it.

Opening it, I look down at the ring.

A little bird, made from diamonds, set on a platinum band.

She will say yes.

Of course, she will say yes.

I tuck the velvet box into my pocket and pull out into the road, driving towards the other side of the city where her little apartment is.

When she comes home, I will be waiting for her. Like I have been waiting so many times in the past - but this time I am going to say hello.

CHAPTER EIGHT
Nerissa

"How are you getting home?" Hayley asks, eyeing me up and down. "There is no way you are driving yourself." She says.

"Don't be silly. I got an Uber here. I will Uber home." I laugh, pulling her towards me to hug her goodbye.

Tonight was magical. It was *almost* perfect.

Friends surrounded me, and they really made it special for me. I can't believe how amazing they all were.

The only thing that dragged me down was the fact that Riley just didn't show up. I don't understand why he couldn't message me or tell me what was going on. But whatever *special* thing he wanted to tell me - he chickened out. For a while now I have suspected that he likes Tabatha, the prettiest girl in the class. I mean, I don't stand a chance against someone as beautiful as her. Any man would choose her over me. I wouldn't blame them.

Hayley dodges my attempt to hug her goodbye and pouts out her bottom lip.

"Can't you stay just a little longer. I'm having so much fun." She grumbles.

"Hayley, you are so bad. Most of the people have left. It's really late. Don't you have work in the morning?" I ask, trying to reason with her. Hayley has a side job in the coffee shop near her apartment. She works most weekends because that is when people tip the most.

"Nope, I took the day off especially so I could party with you *all night loooooong.*" She says with a grin.

"Ok, but it's almost three in the morning. We did party all night." I'm tired.

"One more drink. Just you and me. Not all the other people. Just me and my best friend on her birthday and then you can go home and get into your cozy bed and go to sleep." She is so drunk, and trying hard so I cave to the peer pressure. "Fine, one, that's it."

Hayley waves a waitress over to the VIP table and orders us each a glass of champagne. My head is already spinning less because I stopped drinking about an hour and a half ago. I don't like hangovers. They are a waste of time, and I don't see the point in ever getting that drunk. But this extra glass of champagne won't affect me too much. I'll still wake up fresh tomorrow *if I get enough sleep. Sleep, and hydration — that's the secret.*

Hayley leans into me, tipsy and loving. "You really are my best friend. I don't know where I would be without you."

"I'd be on my way home to bed." I laugh.

She punches me in the arm. "Hey, no jokes. I mean it, Nerissa. You are so inspiring. After everything you went through. You still push so hard to be the best person you can be. You are so beautiful, inside, and outside. I just want you to know that you mean the world to me."

I wrap my arms around my drunk, emotional best friend and hug her tight.

"You are just as special to me, Hayley. This is a two-way street. You are the reason I found my feet and my confidence again. You are basically my sister."

She grins. "If I'm your sister, you can never get rid of me."

I laugh, agreeing with her.

We sit together and finish our last drink, reminiscing over the amusing things that happened during college and how our lives are really about to begin now that we are in the big wide world and getting proper office jobs and all those adult type things.

"I'm sorry Riley flaked on you." Hayley says, pulling her mouth tight. "I'll slap him next time I see him. He doesn't deserve you. Douchecanoe."

I shrug my shoulders, brushing off the pain of his rejection. "It's ok. It just wasn't meant to be."

"We will find you a proper prince charming." She teases.

"I don't think I want a prince charming. I think I just want to work and focus on my future. boys are stupid."

"That's my girl." Hayley says. "Men suck."

"Come on." I pull her to her feet. "I am going to get you an Uber."

She sighs and follows me downstairs. The club is getting a lot emptier. It's definitely home time now.

Once Hayley is inside the Uber, I booked for her and on her way home I book one for myself and wait. It doesn't take long at all because this is a popular part of the city. I'm certain they park around the corner and wait.

I am exhausted and looking forward to a quick shower and a warm bed. I'm not used to wearing these heels, my feet ache, but wow they make my legs look amazing.

I smile as I watch the city lights flash past the window all the way home.

I had an epic night.

I have awesome friends and a bright future ahead of me. This is the life I imagined for myself - I'm living it.

I think of my mom, and how proud she would have been when I graduated. And that I did so well. Maybe tonight, instead of partying, I would have gone to a fancy dinner with her. Something special that we could have treated ourselves to. Celebrating the graduation and my birthday at the same time.

I sigh, looking down at my hands. I miss her so much. Not a day goes by when I don't wish she was still with me.

But I'm doing really well mom. Things are going so well for me. Not with boys, but hey, I was never that good with boys so there isn't anything new there. I chuckle to myself, and the Uber driver eyes me in the rearview mirror.

He pulls up outside my apartment.

Home sweet home.

"Thank you." I say, climbing out and waving goodbye.

He waits until I am inside the building, before he drives away which I think is sweet of him.

I thought I meant something to Riley. Him ditching me tonight stings, even if I am trying not to let it get to me. Who ghosts a girl on her birthday? What the fucking fuck?

I roll my eyes and slip my feet out of my heels to climb the two flights of stairs to my apartment. The elevator has been broken for a while and there is no way my poor feet can handle any more time in these gorgeous shoes.

I just don't get it. I really have shit luck with boys. In fact, he is the third one who just disappeared on me. Ghosted me. I guess I'm just not worth that much to them.

I hate how much it hurts me.

No one likes rejection, But just for once I want to be on the other side of that, to be wanted. To be chosen, wholeheartedly and enthusiastically. I want them to be afraid of losing me, not waiting to be ditched.

Some people go their whole lives wanting to know what that's like. Maybe I am doomed to be one of those lost souls who never knows.

I'll have to get six cats, a weird hobby that requires wool, and a pink fluffy gown so I sit around in my apartment all day.

I laugh, almost at my front door.

"What an awesome night." I say to myself as I slip the key into the door and push it open.

It's so dark, I should have left a light on.

Running my hand along the wall I flick the switch, and bright light floods the small space. It's too much light, after being in the dimly lit club, and because I am so tired, it's just too much. I walk over to my bed, flick on the fairy lights and turn off the big light by the door again.

That's much better. The soft twinkling glitter of the fairy lights is pretty, and it makes my home cozy and special.

Standing in front of my closet and the long mirror on it, I smile.

I don't recognize the woman in the mirror. I don't see myself in that reflection.

The girl standing there, with the glittering short body tight black dress on - she looks beautiful. She might even be sexy. I stand up on my tiptoes, picturing the heels I refuse to put back on and I spin a little to see my dress from different angles.

This dress might just be the start of a new me.

But - if Riley didn't come tonight - then he can't be the one who bought it for me.

I run my hands over the luxurious fabric.

Who in the world got me this dress - and why has no one said anything?

How can I say thank you if I don't even know where it came from?

I'm still dazzled by my reflection.

When I see the shadow of a movement behind, I freeze. There's someone in here. Maybe it's the neighbors cat? Shit. I can't move — I can't breathe.

A tall man steps out from the dark corner behind the armor next to my bed. Was he there this whole time? How the hell didn't I notice? There was a person in my house and I didn't see him, I'm never drinking again.

I still can't move. My heart is beating so fast I'm going to puke, cry and scream at the same time. But none of those things are happening.

I need to scream or run or hide or find a weapon. But I can't move.

He takes another step towards me, my instincts are broken, why am I not doing anything to survive? To live. To get away — to — why — why does he look so familiar?

CHAPTER NINE
Tuomo

I watch her, admiring at herself in the mirror, admiring how beautiful she looks in the dress I bought her. I have never seen a more gorgeous woman in my life, and it feels animalistic to just sit in the dark here, in the corner of her room, admiring that beauty.

That stunning creature that will soon be mine.

I grin, a dark, knowing smile.

My heart is racing with excitement.

Right now, she is mine to do with as I please. I could take her, I could do whatever I wanted. She'd be powerless to stop me.

I shake my head. No. That is not the game I am playing. I am playing a different game tonight. A patient game. A game that in the long run will make her mine forever.

My cock stirs, hardening against my pants as I sit with my legs spread and my chin resting on one hand. My elbow propped on the arm of the chair.

Patience, Tuomo.

You always get what you want in the end, and this will be no different.

She stands up on her tiptoes and turns around in front of the mirror, giving me a better view of the curve of her hip as it dips towards her waist.

Fuck me.

Patience.

Patience.

Patience.

I brush my hand over my cock, wanting it to calm down, but wandering if it is going to be possible until I have tasted her.

But I wait. I wait and I force my body to conform to what I need right now.

She frowns at her reflection and looks worried for a moment and I think she's seen me. But then she runs her hands over the dress.

Oh. I get it.

She wants to know who it's from.

Curiosity is killing her, like patience is killing me.

It is time to put her out of her misery. And me out of mine.

I stand up, as silent and as deadly as a predator. Taking one slow step forward.

She sees me and her eyes grow wide.

Wide and wild and terrified.

She needs a moment to recognize me. Once she does her face will change. She will be happy. She will run into my arms, and we will celebrate being reunited.

I smile, knowing it is a dangerous smile, but unable to hold back.

I take another step closer, so that I am in better light. So, she can see my face. Her mouth drops open, and I see it in her eyes. I can see she knows who I am.

"Hello, little bird." I growl, tilting my chin lower and staring into her eyes in the mirror.

The smallest squeak escapes her lips, and her body shakes.

Then she spins around to face me, while simultaneously taking two steps backwards and landing up with her back pressed against the mirror she was just watching.

"Tu - Tuomo?" She stammers, a breathless whisper that is barely audible.

"Did you miss me?" I purr, as I step closer.

She tries to take another step away from me, but she can't. She's trapped.

I step closer.

I should be offended that she looks so scared, but I am excited by it. I am excited by the idea of hunting her, of claiming her and making her mine.

I shake my head to push the thought away.

No.

Patience. I must have patience.

I stop walking towards her, tilting my head to the side and forcing my face to relax.

"I came to say happy birthday and to see if you liked the gift I got you."

She takes a sharp breath. "Gift?" She is still in shock.

"It looks beautiful on you." I gesture with my eyes, letting them trace up and down her figure.

Realization flashes in her face. She reaches up and touches her stomach, touching the dress.

"The dress." She whispers. "You gave me the dress?"

"I saw you looking at it in the window so many times."

"You saw me?"

Slowly her face is becoming more and more focused, less shocked, less confused.

Her jaw clenches tight, and her brows furrow when she pushes away from the mirror.

"You were following me? And now you are in my apartment? What the fuck is this? What the fuck do you think you are doing?" She's shouting. "I'm calling the police." She lunges for her phone.

I can't have her shouting at me, or calling the cops. I don't want her neighbors hearing and interrupting our reunion.

"Nerissa - it's your birthday."

She throws her hands in the air in frustration. "I *know* it's my birthday. What does that have to do with you trespassing, breaking and entering, fucking stalking?" She is still shouting.

"Lower your voice." I warn her.

She seems to pause for a moment, my tone a clear warning that she understood.

But then her face changes again and yells. "Get the fuck out of my apartment you psychopath." She's seething mad. "You can't just walk in here. You can't just come back into my life. Do you want your stupid dress back? Is that it? You can have it. I don't care." She is tugging at the dress, trying to pull it off her shoulders, but I can't let her do that. If she strips out of that dress, I won't have patience. I won't be able to stop myself.

"Don't, Nerissa. Stop. What the fuck is wrong with you?" I snarl, rushing towards her and grabbing her wrists, then tugging the dress back down.

Her eyes are wide with terror. Why is she so scared of me?

We are in love. We have been in love for years. Why would she fear the person she loves - or the person who loves her?

She kicks me hard, her heel connecting with my shin, and it sends a burst of pure anger through me.

I grab her throat and lift her in the air, spinning her towards the bed, I throw her onto it.

"What the fuck do you think you are doing?" I growl, staring down at her. "Calm down, right now, before you make me do something I will regret."

She scuttles up the bed, away from me, tears streaming down her cheeks.

I don't want her to cry.

I didn't mean to hurt her or make her scared.

This is not how this was supposed to go. She is supposed to be happy to see me.

I touch the velvet box in my pocket, wondering how this went so wrong?

"Nerissa - just calm the fuck down for a second."

Her eyes are red with tears, her cheeks flushed and bright.

"Please just go. I don't want to die. Please, just get out. Please."

"Die?" I say in shock. "I am not here to kill you." I stammer.

"Then get out." She screams so loud I rush to the front door and open it to check if anyone is coming out of the apartments on either side of her. But this is a dodgy part of town, and no one pokes their nose in anyone else's business.

I pull the door shut again, locking it.

When I walk back towards the bed, she is holding a baseball bat, kneeling in the middle of the bed, ready to fight me.

"A bat? Really?" I sigh, reaching forward and as she swings it, I catch it and yank it from her hands.

She stands up on the bed and starts swinging her fists at me.

I grab her around the waist and drop her onto her back, pinning her down with my body. Spreading her legs wide so she can't kick me in the nuts, I pin her arms above her head.

She is crying again, thick streams of salty tears running down her cheeks. My cock is getting harder by the second. Pressed right up against her pussy. The dress hitched up over her hips in the struggle.

This is not what I want.

But fuck me - this is *exactly* what I want.

She can feel me against her, and she takes in a sharp breath. She bites her lower lip so hard I am sure it is going to bleed.

"Stop, calm down. Please. I will not do anything to you." I snark against her cheek.

"You are hurting me." She whimpers, trying to wiggle her wrists free.

"I will let you go if you promise to stop screaming."

She lies dead still for a moment and my body is raging. Every cell in my is telling me to do it. To take her. To take what I have waited so long for.

But it's not the way I planned for this to go.

Finally, she takes a soft breath. "I promise." She whispers.

"You promise not to scream?"

"I promise." She says again, her voice hoarse with tears.

I release her wrists, lifting myself up, resting on my arms which are pressed into the bed on either side of her head. I stare at her for a moment.

The most perfect, most beautiful creature in the world.

Then I clench my jaw and push off her.

"I came here to talk." I say with frustration. "I thought you would be happy to see me."

The disappoint in my voice is not hidden.

When I turn around to look at her, she is leaning over to grab her hoodie from the floor next to the bed. For a moment her ass in the air, facing me.

Then she comes back up and throws it over her head.

I run my fingers through my hair.

Then I pull my mouth tight, look up at the ceiling and take a slow deep breath.

It was a shock. That's all.

She will remember everything when she calms down. And then this will go according to plan.

CHAPTER TEN
Nerissa

He has me pinned to the bed and my heart is racing so fast I can't breathe. His cock is pressed up against my pussy and I can feel how hard he is. The darkness in his eyes tells me I am in danger and the worst part of it - the worst part of it - is that my body wants him.

My pussy throbbing with desire, my body wanting to thrust up against him.

But the tears are falling down my cheeks because I am terrified. I don't know what he plans to do with me. I don't know how dangerous he is - or worse - I *know how dangerous he is*.

When he gets off me, making me promise not to scream, I'm shaking.

"I came here to talk." He says. "I thought you would be happy to see me."

He has his back to me as I tug the dress back down over my hips.

My body still warm with desire but my mind knowing better.

I look around, rushed, scared, desperate, and see my oversized hoodie lying on the floor next to the bed. I lean over to grab it.

I need to hide my body. I need to cover up.

He is watching me when I sit back up on the bed. His eyes are hungry with need. They are dark and menacing.

I watch him too. My eyes locked onto every move he is making.

Honestly, I know that if he wants to - he can do anything he wants to me. I can't fight him. He is almost twice my size. I wouldn't stand a chance.

The thought, to my horror, thrills me.

I push it away, disgusted in myself.

I watch as Tuomo tries to regain some sense of control over this situation.

When he looks down at me again, his eyes are calm. "Can we talk, little bird?"

He asks so politely it seems odd given the circumstances. It's a stupid question since I do not have a choice.

"We - we can talk." I say, moving to the other side of the bed. I know my sweatpants are on the floor and I want them.

"Good." He sighs in relief. "Can I pour us a drink or something?"

"I have nothing to drink." I snap.

"Yes, you do. You have that bottle of wine your friend Hayley left here."

My jaw drops open again. How can he know that?

The same way he knew what dress I liked.

With my feet I find my sweatpants and squat down to grab them - without taking my eyes off Tuomo. I am furious, but there is only one way out of this horrible situation.

I have to play along. Somehow. I need to appease him.

I need to find out what he came here for and why - and then I can get him to leave.

He walks to the kitchen while I tug the pants over my legs. I feel so much better covered up. I look like an idiot with the dress sticking out between the hoodie and the sweatpants, but I couldn't care less right now.

Tuomo pours us each a glass of wine while I hover on the other side of my bed, unsure what to do with myself.

He leans across and hands me the wine, then he chuckles, eyeing me up and down.

"The sweatpants are just as cute as the dress, little bird."

How the fuck is he making jokes now?

I take the wine and take a massive gulp. I need to calm my nerves, so I think straight.

Tuomo takes a seat on the single chair on the other side of the bed. I sit on the edge of the bed.

He hasn't changed much. He looks more rugged, sexier, stronger. His body is more muscular, filled out and - what the fuck. Stop perving. Find out what he wants and get him out of your house.

"What did you want to talk about?" I say, trying to sound polite, but my voice is shaking.

"Us. Of course. I have been waiting, and now you are twenty-five. You are not in love. You are not married." He pulls a small velvet box out of his pocket. "Little bird, this is not the way I imagined tonight would go. But I came here to ask you to marry me. It's time." He leans forward in the chair, and he puts the box onto the bed in front of me, the lid open.

He's fucking crazy—or I drank so much I'm hallucinating. I don't say anything but I'm sure my face is saying a lot of stuff.

My eyes drop to the ring in the box.

A beautiful little bird, created out of sparkling stones, set into a ring - it is glittering in the fairy lights. Mesmerized for a moment.

"Remember, I told you that next time I saw you I would give you a real one."

"A real one?" I stammer.

"Yes." He says, standing up suddenly and marching over to my dressing table. He yanks the top drawer open and pulls out a box. A box that is very special to me and filled with memories of my mother - of the Vece mansion - yes - but only because it reminds me of my mother.

He opens the lid and takes out a small plastic bird charm.

He sets the box back down and tosses the charm onto the bed next to the diamond ring.

The little bird. The bird he gave me.

I barely remember it. I know he gave it to me, but the bird was more a symbol of a new beginning for me - in my mind it has nothing to do with him. I had it in my pocket the day I left the Vece mansion. The day I started my new life. It was my wings to fly away.

I pick it up and twist it in my fingers.

"Oh." I say, unsure what to do. "But - what is this?" I touch the box.

"It is your engagement ring. We are going to get married." He says with a smile that runs pins and needles down my spine.

"I am not marrying you." I blurt out, gripping the plastic bird so hard it is spiking into my palm. "I will never marry you."

His eyes grow dark with anger. "You promised. We made a promise to each other. When you turned twenty-five, we were going to get married. It was a pact, Nerissa." He snarls and hisses in anger.

"A pact made by a child. I didn't take it seriously. I haven't even thought about you since that day, Tuomo. I don't even know who you are. I never did. All I know is that you and your family are all monsters. You stole my brothers from me. My mother died in your house. You are just like your father. I would never marry someone like you. I know what your family does. You are evil. You hurt people. You are—"

He flies at me and clamps his hand over my mouth.

"How dare you say that? How dare you compare me to my father? I am nothing like him." The fury in his eyes is a death sentence for me if I make one more wrong move.

I nod against his hand, tears spilling down my cheeks again.

I need to pull myself together.

This is not a game, I better not aggravate him even more.

I reach up and touch his hand, locked so tightly over my mouth that it is hurting.

I run my fingers over his skin, and his grip loosens.

He drops his hand away, but his eyes are still locked into mine.

"I'm sorry. I didn't mean - You aren't like your father." I whisper, hoping I am saying the right thing.

He nods. "It's ok. I forgive you, little bird." He sits down on the bed next to me.

Tuomo reaches up and brushes his fingers across my cheek, wiping away a tear. "I am sorry I made you cry, little bird. I came here because I love you. I never stopped loving you. You don't mean it when you say you haven't thought about me since that day. We made a pact, and we have to honor that pact. It's the only way to stay true to ourselves. We are meant to be together." He's delusional, completely nuts. He's got to know that he sounds crazy.

I bite down on my lip and feel the ache as a bruise forms inside my mouth. I need to stop doing that.

"Tuomo, I mean - that was long ago. So much has changed since then. You don't know who I am anymore. You might not even like the person I grew in to. And I don't know who you are. We can't just get married. It would be stupid, and reckless of us."

It sounds reasonable, everything I am saying is logical, but his eyes tell me he hates every word spilling from my mouth. I'm making him mad.

He swallows hard and looks away for a second.

Thinking.

Plotting.

Deciding.

My heart is racing with fear.

My hands are shaking.

How can I get him to leave?

He stands up from the edge of the bed and starts pacing around my small apartment. I have agitated him again. Fuck. This is not good.

I glance at my window, wondering how high the second story is and if I could jump out of it and not kill myself.

CHAPTER ELEVEN
Tuomo

Nerissa is terrified of me. Her body is rigid, and tense and her eyes give away her emotions too clearly for her own good. She should learn to hold back on letting people see so much about her. I had to learn.

I don't want her to hide anything from me. I want to know everything. I want her deepest darkest fears and her biggest dreams.

I pace up and down her apartment, filled with rage, fuming from her rejection.

Who the fuck does she think she is? Calling me a monster. Comparing me to my father.

If she wasn't the love of my life, I would have to teach her a lesson.

I can't believe I have pictured this night over and over again and not in any - not even one - of those fantasies did I imagine she would reject me. Never mind her call me a monster on top of it.

I grit my teeth, pacing. Up and down. Each step a soothing rhythm as I try to clear my thoughts. Trying to ease away the harsh rejection.

It is only because she is scared. That is the only reason she is saying such horrendous things about me. She doesn't mean it. She would never speak that way about the man she promised to marry when she turned twenty-five.

A monster.

I shake my head.

Don't think about it.

I should make her pay.

My eyes trace over her body, hidden beneath the loose fit of her hoodie. But I know what she looks like under there. I should make her pay. I should take what she owes me. What she made me wait so long to experience.

My cock stirs.

Stop.

Don't think about it. She is special.

She is unique, and she deserves more than that.

I turn to face her again. I am calm. I am focused. I can do this.

"So, you are breaking your promise. You are not going to follow through with the pact we made?" I say.

She takes in a sharp breath. "Tuomo — I'm sorry, I just can't—" I hold up my hand to silence her.

I shake my head and narrow my eyes towards her. My father taught me how to look disappointed.

"Fine." I say.

Her eyes widen.

"Fine?" She asks, tentative and cautious.

"Yes. I agree. It was - it was so long ago. I don't know what I was thinking. Of course, we should get to know each other. We should spend some time together." I laugh, shrugging my shoulders.

"Um - yes." She nods, looking nervous.

I sit down on the bed again, a relaxed posture and a smile on my face.

"Let me take you on a date. Three weeks from now. I'm sorry about how I pushed in here and came across like a crazy person. I just - I wanted to surprise you and it backfired." I chuckle.

"You just wanted to surprise me?" She asks, her brows knotted.

"Yeah, I really messed it up, didn't I?" I grin at her, knowing she always loved my smile.

Slowly a nervous smile spreads across her lips. She pulls her mouth to the side and tilts her head. She looks ever so slightly more relaxed. Good. This is working. Keep going. You have her.

"You really did mess it up." She giggles.

Fuck. It makes me want to kiss her. That musical sound escaping her lips, the way her eyes glitter when she laughs.

No. Have patience. We have a backup plan.

"So, go on a date with me." I say. "I promise to be the perfect gentleman. And you need to accept my apology for how things went down tonight."

She nods.

She locks her eyes onto me.

This is how it works. If a person says no to something big - then they are much more likely to say yes to the next question if it is something smaller - more reasonable.

She is watching my every move. Paying careful attention to my expressions and my body language. I can tell she wants me. I can tell she would love it if I just took her right now on her bed. The bed I have watched her play with herself on. The bed I have dreamed of fucking her on. I run my hands over the duvet, my eyes still locked on hers. My fingers touching the fabric that has been wrapped around her body night after night.

"Ok. I will go on a date with you. But it's just a date, Tuomo. It doesn't mean that we are going to get married or anything like that. Just one date. Ok?" She says, trying to gain control over everything again.

"Of course, it is just a date and a chance for us to spend a little time together. If it goes well - I hope, we can have another. But I understand - this is the trial. This is our chance to catch up and learn who we are again." I nod.

She nods.

We stare at each other for a long time and the air between us is sharp with static electricity. I feel as though I could reach out and touch her and a thread of lighting would connect us.

I pull my eyes away from her.

Just a date.

A date that is going to spark a chain of events that she has no idea has already been planned out. The moment she said no to me. The moment she rejected me and broke her promise. Everything that I put together as my back-up plan became the primary plan.

Just a date - yes - but so much more.

Three weeks.

There are two reasons I have set it so far in the future. The first is that I want to give her some time to get over the shock of me returning into her life. I think, just maybe, if she takes the time to think about everything, she might decide to do the right thing and keep her promise to me. She might make the right decision. Three weeks is enough time for her to have the space to do that.

However, three weeks is also long enough for her body to adjust.

Because I have switched out her birth control pills. I have changed them for almost identical looking sugar pills. She won't know the difference. She will take them every day for the next three weeks but come the night of our date - she will not be in any type of birth control and that is when I can carry out my plan.

If she rejects me again, I will ruin her life.

I will make sure that every plan for the future that she has falls apart.

She will beg me to give her another chance because she will have nothing and no one else.

Because if I can't have her - no one can.

But I am getting ahead of myself now.

I am sure she will come to her senses over the next three weeks.

I am sure she will realize what she needs to do. The right thing to do.

"Can I get you another glass of wine?" I ask, standing up and reaching over the bed to her side table and picking up her glass. My body brushes close to hers and she goes rigid.

I scoop the small velvet box into my hand as well, shoving it back into my pocket.

"I really need to get some sleep. It's been a long night." She says.

"Nonsense. It's your birthday. You should celebrate the entire night. If you were my girl, I would have whisked you away to some tropical island and we would have drunk cocktails on the beach all day, letting the sun kiss our skin red."

I chuckle, walking back to the kitchen.

I pour is each another glass of wine and carry it back to her.

I can see she is still scared but trying so hard to hide it from me.

I am still turned on her fear. I feel like I am in full control of everything happening right now.

She sips her wine, not speaking, not moving much either. I watch her. Thinking about our future together.

When her wine glass is empty, she stands up. She forces a bold look on her face as she smiles at me.

"Thank you for - um - for the surprise. It was nice to see you again."

I stand up too.

She walks towards her door and pulls it open.

I follow her at a slow pace.

I lean close to her, pushing her back against the open doorframe.

"You are even more beautiful than the first day I saw you. You seem to be alive, more gorgeous, more enticing with each passing year. Never forget how beautiful you are, little bird." I wrap my hand around her jaw and tilt her face up towards mine.

I press my lips against hers, expecting her to jerk her head away in horror, but she doesn't. She freezes in place as my lips play across hers.

She lets me kiss her, forcing my tongue inside her mouth. She lets me kiss her passionately.

When I step away, I am grinning - and my cock is hard again. But I hide it this time.

She stands in her doorway, shivering, watching me walk away.

I'll see you again soon my little bird.

I can't wait.

CHAPTER TWELVE
Nerissa

I stand in the doorway for ages. Frozen from fear and shock. I have already watched long enough to see him disappear down the stairway, out of sight. I listened as his footsteps faded all the way to the ground floor. But I still can't move myself from this doorframe.

My eyes are still glued to the end of the passage.

I am so terrified I can't move.

From somewhere in my little apartment my phone buzzes as I receive a message.

I jump in fright, snapped out of my stupor. I close the door and lock it.

I can't believe that just happened.

Tuomo Vece was in my apartment. He was here. He was - he pinned me to the bed - he - he kissed me.

I lift my hand and touch my fingers to my lips. He kissed me.

When I was young, his kiss was the most exciting thing I had ever experienced in my entire life.

But I was naïve back then. I didn't understand he was an actual monster of a man from a monstrous family.

I sigh, walking towards my bed to find my phone.

Now, I am old enough to see the truth about who he is, but his kiss *still* shook me to my core. I've kissed other men - but it has never felt like that.

I think, perhaps, it is just the sense of danger. The adrenaline in my veins. The fear in my heart. That's all it was.

I sit on my bed, facing the door because I am too scared to turn my back to it.

I flick my phone on and navigate to the messages to see who is sending me things at four in the morning.

> Tuomo: Turn off your light and go to sleep, little bird. I will see you at Restaurant Du Mort on the seventeenth at eight o'clock. Night, beautiful girl.

I stare at the message. And somehow, I know he is looking through my bedroom window. He is down there, in the street, perhaps sitting in his car, and he is looking at my bedroom window.

I should check, but I'm too scared.

Instead, I reach over and switch my light off. Then I sit with my legs curled against my chest and the blankets wrapped around me, unable to sleep. Barely able to move.

I can't believe what just happened.

I can't believe he was in my apartment.

How many times has he been in here? He knew exactly where the wine was, and where the glasses were. Even where my little memory box was. He knew which dress I had been admiring in the shop window.

I bite my bottom lip, sinking down into my bed.

I am so tired I feel like my bones are aching from it.

I think I will never sleep again, but it's been a long night and sleep steals me away much faster than I could have imagined.

I wake up the next morning with a fright. Rolling over and throwing the blankets off and looking around my entire apartment.

But Tuomo isn't there.

As the days go by, I do not see him anywhere. I keep a sharp look out for him, but he isn't there.

It's strange, because it's like he is everywhere - watching me all the time - his eyes on me and that dark smile curling up at the corners as he spies on me.

But I think I am just paranoid after finding him in my bedroom.

The shock is wearing off though and as the days go by and I don't see him I feel more and more at ease.

Maybe it was just a stupid attempt at a surprise. Maybe he really didn't have any intensions of scaring me.

But - no - I know better than that. I shouldn't play it down. I shouldn't make excuses for him.

His family is dangerous. I can't forget that.

The Vece family always gets what they want, no matter who they have to walk over to make it happen.

That's why - and I concluded after a lot of thought, that is why I have to go on the date.

If I go on the date, then I have kept my word. And in a public, safe place, I can try to talk some reason into him. My bedroom, at past three in the mooring, after terrifying the living daylight out of me - was not a good place.

But in a restaurant filled with people and noise and atmosphere - I am sure I can get him to see reason and understand that we are from different worlds.

Ugh.

It doesn't help that I still think he is the hottest guy on the planet.

In fact - yes - he got hotter and it's an enormous problem trying to stay focused around him.

But looks isn't everything. His heart is dark. And stained with his family's blood. Generations of dangerous men that I want nothing to do with.

So, I will go on the date. But that is it.

After that I am done with him.

I won't agree to a second date. In fact, I hope I never see him again.

After the date my new job will be starting and everything in my life will fall into place. I will focus on my career and not have to worry about Tuomo - or any men for that matter. I can just focus on me.

As the weeks pass by my sense of security increases. I am relaxed and confident that it was just a stupid misunderstanding. I spend time with Hayley, and I learn about the new company I am going to be working for. I'm happy and confident and excited.

Now and then I get a shudder down my spine, and an icy shiver over my neck it's like someone is watching me - but I know I am just being paranoid. Especially someone like Tuomo. He is way too busy to be sneaking around all day following me. He has a life. He has a business. He has a family.

It's just ridiculous to think that he is stalking me.

I can't help but glance around me when I get that strange sensation, it prickles my skin.

I never see him. I never expect to either. I just - I have to check.

As the night of our date gets closer, I think about Tuomo more.

I remember who he is, how he treated me. I remember his father, his brothers, and how terrified I was of them. Tuomo was like this forbidden, mysterious temptation. He isn't that anymore. He's very real and very dangerous now. There is nothing mysterious about him and I need to keep my guard up.

One date.

I will play nice.

I will be friendly.

And then I will never see him again because he will find out how boring I am.

I mean - that's what's happening here. He also remembers me as this forbidden girl. The girl his father told him never to be with. He has some kind of idea in his head about me and I know I am not that person. I am not that exciting or that beautiful. He just needs to spend time with me to realize that there are hundreds - thousands - of girls in this city ten times prettier than I am.

He can have any of them. His family is infamous. Girls probably fall all over him every day.

I nod to myself as I leave my apartment, walking down to the little cafe on the corner to get some milk for my tea. I shove my hands into my baggy jeans pockets and focus on what's ahead of me so that I can ignore the creepy sensation of being watched again.

One date.

He will see the real me.

It will all be over.

He will ghost me just like every single other boy who ever showed an interest in me since as long as I can remember.

CHAPTER THIRTEEN
Tuomo

Swopping the birth control pills out was easy.

I did it the night of her birthday before she got home. If she had said yes to my proposal of marriage, I would have swapped them back, but she said no - and now she will have to deal with the consequences of breaking that promise.

I have been watching her over the past few weeks since her birthday.

I have been waiting for her to change her mind about saying no - about calling me a monster - about her poor choices.

But she hasn't. In fact, very little has changed, and she seems to go on about her daily life as before.

The only thing that is different is that she often looks around herself now. A little more aware. A little more alert.

She senses I'm watching her. But she can't prove it. I am too good at what I do. I have been following her for years without her knowing. She won't suddenly see me now.

My obsession with her is mixed with a new anger. A need for revenge against her harsh rejection. She didn't realize it then - but saying no to me doesn't change a fucking thing. I will have her. She will be mine. I will get what I want because I always do - it will just take a little longer and she might not appreciate the methods I choose to make it happen.

She had a chance though. I gave her that.

And now we are doing it my way.

I have been watching the calendar and keeping track of her cycles. Our date falls exactly when I need it to.

It is going to be perfect.

I see her glancing over her shoulder as she steps out onto the street in front of her apartment. She looks nervous. Then she turns her face forward and walks with determination towards the little cafe down the road. I guess she ran out of something.

My phone vibrates in my pocket, and I sigh, pulling it out to see which of my annoying brothers is calling me.

Rufino.

I clench my jaw as I answer.

"What." I snap.

"Where the fuck are you?" He snaps back at me.

"Out."

"Well, stop fucking around and get back to the house before father sends someone out to drag you back here. He wants to meet with all of us."

I sigh.

Even after I moved into an apartment in the city. Even though I don't work for my father anymore and I have my own branch of the business - even though I am doing everything in my power to distance myself from him - he still has control over me and my brothers.

We all just bow down to him as though he is the king and ruler of the universe.

He's a fucking monster. She was right.

I am nothing like him.

"I'll be there soon." I sigh into the phone.

"Good." Rufino says, then hangs up on me. I slip the phone back into my pocket, watching her walk further down the road. I want to follow, but family duties are calling. I will only make it harder for myself, more complicated, if I don't do as my father asks and go to whatever urgent meeting he has set up.

Soon, I won't have to watch her from a distance. Soon she will be in my arms, and I will have the rest of my life to show her how much I love her.

I start the engine of my car only when she is out of sight.

Revving I push it into gear and pull out onto the road, heading towards my father's mansion.

It's strange to hate someone so much, but I do. I hate him to the point where just a photograph of his face turns my stomach.

I take twenty minutes to get to the house. There wasn't any traffic even though at this time of the day it should have been gridlocked. I would have preferred traffic. To delay arriving here.

Anything to avoid being close to my father.

I climb out of the car and walk up the stone steps of his mansion.

I grew up here - and in all my time in this house - the only thing I enjoyed was her.

"You took your fucking time." Masaccio snaps when I walk in.

"Whatever, I'm here." I wave my hand in the air to dismiss him. The golden boy.

Rufino walks through carrying a cup of coffee.

"Another one?" Celso quips, rolling his eyes. "You don't think you've had enough caffeine to power the city yet?"

"Hey, this asshole was taking forever and I'm hungry." Rufino huffs, sipping the coffee.

"Will you all just shut up." Masaccio complains, rubbing his head.

"Where the fuck are your manners bro?" Celso laughs.

"Where the fuck is your mother, bro?" Masaccio snarls back, moody and dark.

Celso falls deathly silent with rage lines furrowing his face.

His mother is not my mother.

In fact, he doesn't share the same mother as any of us. Our father had a brief fling, and his mother dumped him here and disappeared. He is bitter about it - and even though I don't get on with any of my brothers - that was a low blow for Mas to use against him.

I sit down on the sofa in the living room and chuckle. "If anyone was going to be accused of having a different mother, you'd think it would be red-haired Rufino. The soulless ginger." I taunt to take the pressure off Celso and Mas's nasty comment.

But it wasn't a good choice because Rufino isn't just hungry - he's hangry. He's the biggest of all of us and when he gets hungry - he gets fucking moody.

He spins towards me with a snarl on his face. His dark red hair is like flames as though he has risen from hell to rain scorn upon my soul.

I hold my hands up.

"Dude, I'm kidding. Can someone give him a snickers bar or something?"

"Finally." My father's voice booms into the living room, and we all jump to attention.

He walks in and sits down on the far sofa. His usual spot.

"Sit, for fuck sakes I haven't got all day." He snaps at my brothers.

My father drones on about the new product we are incorporating into our shipments, and I feel my insides roll over. We've already had this meeting. We've had it twice. We have prepared for the new product until our eyeballs were floating in information about it.

Yes, it ships tomorrow. Yes, we are ready. Why the fuck are we wasting our time talking about it still.

"Tuomo?" His deep voice snaps me to attention.

I look towards him. His eyes are right on me. I didn't fucking hear what he said.

"Are we interfering with your busy schedule? Do you have somewhere better to be?" his sarcasm is rich.

"No, why?" I say, holding back any attitude I want to throw in his direction.

"Do you want to take part or at least pay attention then?" he snaps.

I nod. Clenching my jaw shut to stay silent. There is rarely any point in disagreeing with my father. It never goes well. So, when you do it - you better have a fucking reason.

For the rest of the meeting, I sit forward in my seat, resting my elbows on my knees with my hands folded in front of me. I focus.

Not because I want to. But because I want this to go smoothly so I can get back out there and see what Nerissa is up to.

The meeting ends. As pointless as I thought it would be.

Rufino heads straight to the kitchen, Masaccio flicks the television on, and I walk straight out of the door.

"See you guys later." I say, not waiting for their response.

I need to get back to Nerissa.

The morning of our date arrives, and I wake up eager. But I am impatient, checking the time throughout the day and wanting it to move faster - to be eight o'clock.

After I've shown my face at work and got everything, I need to do done I head over to Nerissa's apartment.

She inside, standing by the mirror on her closet. She is holding dresses up against her body, trying to decide which one to wear.

I watch her with fascination - wondering what she is thinking.

She is trying to look pretty for our date.

She wants to grab my attention.

I guess she has come around and perhaps remembered just how close we used to be.

Well, even if she hasn't remembered, she will soon. She will have no choice because I am going to manipulate her world to the point of no return. She will have no choice but to be with me.

Especially when she falls pregnant with my baby.

She will be trapped without a choice.

She will be mine.

I smile. Not wanting to drive away, but I need to go home and shower and get ready as well.

Tonight, everything will fall into place.

CHAPTER FOURTEEN
Nerissa

I keep sighing. Heavy and frustrated and nervous and anxious and wondering what the hell I am doing.

I hold another dress up against my body and stare at my reflection in the mirror.

I don't feel pretty today, but I want to put in some effort for the restaurant we are going to. I have never been there, but I've read about it. It's over the top extravagant.

I toss the blue dress aside and hold the red one up.

I roll my eyes and throw my hands in the air, sending the dress flapping after my gesture.

"What the hell is wrong with me?" I say out loud.

I'm just worried.

I shouldn't even be going on this date. It's a terrible idea.

Tuomo is a dangerous man, and I shouldn't be involved with him on any level.

Ok, but I don't really have a choice. I have to do this - get him off my back - let him see I'm not some fantasy that he has built me into over the years - I'm just *me*. That's all.

I turn back to the mirror and hold the red dress up again. It's the prettiest of all of them I have looked at so far.

It's long, with a high slit that runs to my hip. I've only worn it once, and I was super self-conscious in it the entire time. But tonight is an elegant place and I must wear an elegant dress.

I don't want to wear the flowery blue one and he's already seen me in the black sequin one - that he got me - and the only other dress I own is a little too big for me.

So, fine. The red dress it is.

With the choice made I hop into the shower. It's still early but blow drying my hair is a tedious task and it takes forever, so I need to get going on that now.

By seven thirty, when I look in the mirror, I don't recognize myself.

I am looking at that confident girl who wore the black dress.

I grin.

I like her.

I enjoy being her.

It's strange how a dress and some make-up can elevate your self-esteem. Is this what all the pretty girls do? Are they all just like *me* when you wipe off their make up?

I spin in front of the mirror, admiring how the dress flows out over my ass and how the slit teases the eye a bit, almost revealing my hip bone. I had to wear a G-string that sits high on my hips. I'm not used to it, and I hope it doesn't annoy me all night.

I considered not wearing any underwear at all because I think the dress is worn that way, but I wouldn't dare. That's just not me.

I order an Uber on my phone and then hurry downstairs because it says it's only a minute away.

I guess this is it. There is no backing out now.

Have dinner. Be polite. Let him down gently. Go home. Then this will all be over.

※

Walking into Restaurant Du' Mort I am in awe of how beautiful the place is.

It is classy and extravagant, and I have to stop my mouth from hanging open as I walk through the reception area into the main dining room.

The hostess leads me to the table where Tuomo is waiting. He stands as soon as he sees me and shakes his head while his eyes graze over my body. He has a wide smile on his face. "Each time I think you can't get any more beautiful than the last time I saw you - you keep proving me wrong." He says, holding out his hand.

I place my hand in his and he pulls me towards him, kissing my cheek.

Tuomo pulls my chair out and then tucks it in again behind me. As he walks around to his side of the table, I steal a look at his ass, and the way his pants hug his thick, muscular legs.

He sits down and shifts his chair around the table to be closer to me.

Our legs are almost touching, but not quite. I can feel the heat of his body in proximity to mine. It is distracting me, and I pick up the menu to focus on something else.

"Have you ever been here before, little bird?" Tuomo asks, his eyes on me. I shift in my seat, taking a breath and reminding myself it's just one date.

"No." I giggle. "The places I go to are very different from this."

He smiles. "I can make recommendations off the menu for you. I eat here often so I've tried quite a few of their dishes. I know which ones are sure to leave you *satisfied*."

He raises his brow at me, tilting his head ever so slightly. He's flirting, but at least he's being subtle. A lot more subtle that insisting we get married after not seeing each other for six years.

Nothing on the menu makes sense to me anyway, and I am already overwhelmed just being here with him so, I decide to give him the lead. "Well, then I trust you to order us something amazing." Closing the menu, I push it away from myself.

Tuomo orders champagne for us, and while we sip it, he tells me a little about his life and his business. He keeps things vague, and I know why. His business is not public knowledge for a reason. Oh sure, the cover business is - but not his real one. And his life, with his family - well, let's just say they have always been secretive so why would that change now.

"What about you, little bird?"

"What about me?" the champagne bubbles are tingling through my blood, relaxing me.

"What made you study law?"

"Mm. I think it was because I like the idea of standing up for people who can't stand up for themselves."

"It's because you have a soft heart, and you care about people. I have always admired that about you."

"I'm not as noble as you think I am. I also did it because I want a good life for myself. I want to make something of myself."

"Yes, you are driven - another thing I like about you. You focus on what you want, and you make sure you get it. You and I are a lot alike in that way."

I want to hate him, I want to not be attracted to him, but the more we talk the more I lean towards him. Tonight, he is nothing like the man I fought off in my apartment. He is attentive and showering me in compliments.

Throughout my life I have struggled to accept compliments, because I know I am not pretty, but he is noticing all the other things about me - my strengths. My academic achievements and my heart.

It's as though he is seeing me for who I am and it's making me feel far more special than it should.

I really do need to be careful.

I know who his family is. I know who he is.

Tuomo pours me another glass of champagne as the food arrives.

He ordered two giant platters with of samples of everything.

"Tuomo, this is so much food." I laugh.

"I talked the chef into making this just for us. A sample of all of my favorite things on the menu. This way - you can try everything and next time we come here you'll know what you like."

"Next time." I grin but lower my face to hide it from him.

I should slow down with the champagne. In my mind it's easy to blame those delightful little bubbles for my lapsing sense of judgment. But it's just me - and how gorgeous he looks tonight - and how he is making me smile.

"Why didn't you ever have a boyfriend, little bird? Were you saving yourself for me?"

He asks with a grin, but somewhere inside me my instincts tell me he really believes I was saving myself for him. That isn't the case at all. I tried to have boyfriends, but they all ended up ghosting me.

Shrugging my shoulders I pick up my champagne glass and take a sip. "I guess I just didn't find a man who was manly enough to stick around."

"They are all fools. Those are boys, not men." His eyes are burning into me. Dark brown, like chocolate pools. They're divine. I want to look away, but I can't. Instead, I smile, and bite my lower lip, knowing that I am being demure. I can see how his eyes grow darker when I do it. It is the first time a guy has looked at me this way and it's incredible.

Tuomo adds a few other delights to my side plate and sounds really excited when he tells me to try the halloumi cheese deep fried in sesame seeds and secret spices.

He looks like a child when he gets excited. Like something hidden inside him that shines through. I stare at him, wondering if he ever lets anyone else see this side of him.

CHAPTER FIFTEEN
Tuomo

The moment she walked in wearing that red dress I was set in my decision that no matter what happened tonight I would have her. She would give herself to me.

Dinner started with her being a little cold, distant and protective of herself, but I have played it cool. And while I positioned myself next to her, I am not the one who pressed our legs together beneath the table - she is.

And I am not the one who is leaning in towards me while I speak.

It's easy to compliment such an enticing creature. She is beautiful, I could tell her in a thousand ways how she could compete with every sunset and night sky to hold my attention.

Honestly, I'm doing my best to hold back a little. To not smother her in words that end up overwhelming her and making her think I am being fake.

Nothing about what I tell her is fake. I mean every word.

She giggles, holding her hand in front of her mouth as though she is shy to laugh. I reach out and take her hand, lowering it from her face.

"Your smile is so beautiful, don't hide it. You should never hide anything about yourself from me."

Her cheeks flush pink and she rubs her lips together, smoothing the lip-gloss she has just put on. I watch her mouth, thinking about all the things I want to do with those lips.

When she picks up her fork to taste another sample of food, I top up her champagne. I have made sure, throughout the evening, to keep her glass full. That way she doesn't keep track of how many glasses she's had, and she won't notice when it all hits her at once.

It is lowering her guard and softening the high walls she has built against me.

"I've missed you, Nerissa. I missed you a lot when you left the mansion. You were the only good thing about that place." My heart pulls tight because my words are too emotional. I didn't mean to share that much. Men aren't supposed to be so emotional. My father always told me that. Wincing at my stupidity I look away from her, picking up my drink to take a sip. Trying to act casual. I clear my throat.

She has said nothing, and I can't resist the curiosity growing inside me, so I glance at her.

Her eyes are soft and warm, full of care. She reaches out and takes my hand beneath the table.

"You had a tough life at the mansion, Tuomo. I'm sorry that you had to go through that. I'm glad that I could make you smile back then - and now."

I turn towards her.

She is relaxed, and this is the perfect moment. I reach up and trace my fingers across her cheek, then wrap my hand around the back of her neck. She doesn't move, her eyes are still on me. I pull her closer as I lean towards her.

My lips touch hers and fireworks erupt inside me.

My heart beats faster and my breathing becomes heavy.

Kissing her is like heaven.

I wonder what the rest of her body will be like to touch.

When she leans away from me, she is blushing. In a shy gesture she tucks a strand of hair behind her ear and looks down at the table.

I lift her chin with my finger, making her look up. "I bet every single man in this place is wishing that he could do that to you." I whisper and she giggles.

"Why do you like me, Tuomo? I - I don't understand. You could have anyone. You were in that magazine one - *the most elegible bachelor in the city* - I saw the article. There are hundreds of girls after you."

A dark chuckle rumbles from my chest. "You don't get it do you? A hundred girls could throw themselves at me and I won't even notice. There is only one girl who has ever had my attention. It's always been that way."

Her eyes are deep pools of curiosity. Hazel and gold and filled with a longing to believe what I'm telling her. She really does not know what she means to me - or how beautiful she is. All my years of chasing other guys away from her has benefited me. She doesn't believe any of them wanted her.

"Come have dessert at my place. Or coffee. Or another drink. Come and talk to me some more. I'm not ready to end this night yet." I say, reaching out and taking her hand.

Nerissa is quiet for a moment, then she nods, and my excitement grows. Step by step my plan is working. I am getting her exactly where I want her. She is eating out of my hand.

I stand up and guide her to her feet. The slit of her dress falls open over her legs and my body thunders with need.

After settling the bill, I lead her to my car. She climbs in and I close the door behind her.

I can't believe I am getting what I want.

All those years of patience and she is going to be mine.

At my penthouse she walks around admiring the art and simple clean decor while I admire her narrow waist and wide hips.

She turns to face me, wanting to ask a question and gasps when she realizes how close I am to her. I reach out and touch her waist, dragging her against my chest.

Nerissa looks up at me, her eyes wide, her lips parted.

Before she can say anything, I kiss her.

She sinks into my arms, letting go of any resistance and giving in to me.

Running my hands down her back I trace the curve of her spine, enjoying the shape of her body.

She is nervous, unsure what to do, but that's fine. I know how to make her feel incredible. I know what she wants, and she won't have to worry about a thing.

I slip my hands into the slit of her dress. She moans against my mouth and my cock throbs as I cup my hands over her ass.

Her hands are beneath my shirt, running up my back, tracing over my muscles.

Her breathing is fast and heavy.

I know she wants this.

Tugging the thin straps of her dress off her shoulders I let it slip over her body and fall to the floor at our feet.

She is wearing red lace underwear, no bra, only a transparent G-string that sets my skin on fire with lust.

I can't wait anymore.

I grab her ass and lift her into my arms, wrapping her legs around my waist I press her back against the wall in the passage outside my bedroom.

Tugging my belt open I free my cock.

She moans again when it's rubbing against her pussy. Nothing but the thin lace between us. I tug it aside.

She has never been with a man, she is pure and innocent and saved - just for me.

I push my cock inside her. I watch her expression as I spread her pussy open, inch by inch. She shudders in my arms, digging her nails into my shoulder.

"Does it hurt, little bird?"

She nods, and I dark smile spreads across my face. "It will only hurt the first time. I promise."

I push in harder.

She cries out as I bury myself deep inside her.

I wait for a moment, feeling her pussy pulse over my cock. It takes everything I have to stop myself from moving.

When her body relaxes, I fuck her, moving in and out of her as pleasure floods through me.

I grab a handful of her hair and pull her head back, exposing her neck. I brush my lips across her heated skin, following the dip of her shoulder. Goosebumps form along her neck and I bite her. I want to leave a mark on her, a bruise, a scratch - some kind of evidence to tell the world that she belongs to me now.

Nerissa moans loudly and grips tighter onto my neck so I move faster, pushing harder and deeper.

She arches her back towards me, clamping her thighs around my waist.

"That's it, little bird, let me have you." I growl against her ear.

Her body shakes she is close to coming.

I slip my hand between her legs and press my thumb against her clit. I stroke in small circles and her eyes roll back.

Her pussy tightens around my cock, and she cries out when she orgasms.

I thrust deep inside her as I explode into her pussy.

She will carry my baby.

I will make sure of it.

When we both catch our breath, I lower her to the floor. But I am not done with her.

For my plan to work I need to fuck her again.

I take her hand and lead her to my bedroom.

It is late when we fall asleep with her head resting on my chest and a dark smile on my face. It doesn't matter if she wants to see me again or not - when she finds out she is pregnant she will have no choice.

CHAPTER SIXTEEN
Nerissa

The warmth of the morning sunshine on my face, drags me awake.

At first it's pleasant, but then the headache registers and I groan.

I open my eyes, blinking a few times trying to place my surroundings.

Oh crap.

Everything clicks into place when all the grogginess of sleep fades away in a panicked instant.

I'm lying on my side with my back to Tuomo. His arm is wrapped around my waist.

Shit.

Dammit.

What did I do?

The problem is that I know exactly what I did. I remember everything. Despite the raging headache from drinking too much I wasn't so drunk that I can blame my stupid choices on the alcohol. I knew exactly what I was doing. Slowly lifting my head, I turn to look at him. He's fast asleep still.

I need to get out of here.

I can't handle any kind of conversation with him this morning. Last night I fell for everything he said - hook, line, and sinker.

All of my plans to have dinner and get home as quickly as possible faded the longer I stayed, because I *enjoyed it*.

Dinner was amazing. He was the perfect gentleman, and he made me feel more beautiful than I have felt in my life.

I drag the blankets off my side of the bed, lifting his arm so that I can sneak away from him without disturbing him. I put his arm back down on the bed and wrap the blankets over him. Then I grab my dress, panties, and heels and rush out of the room.

In the living room I get dressed in a hurry, glancing at the bedroom door, terrified that he will come out at any moment.

Where is my phone? I search the area around myself trying to remember what I did with it.

Oh, thank goodness, it's on the kitchen counter. I must have left it there when he started kissing me.

Wow, that kiss was like nothing I had ever experienced before - in fact the entire night was pleasurable that my body is still tingling with delight.

I press my fingers against my eyes.

I lost my virginity. To Tuomo Vece.

I am such an idiot.

But the worst part is that if I had to go back in time I would do it all over again. It was *incredible*.

But it can't happen again.

Double checking that I have everything I walk towards his front door, pulling it open, sneaking out and closing it behind myself. I breathe a sigh of relief outside in the hallway.

In the elevator, riding down the foyer, I book an Uber and keep telling myself that it's all fine.

Everything is going to be fine because I had fun, I don't regret what happened, I just have to be careful with how I handle things in the future.

But I'm convinced that Tuomo got what he wanted. The fantasy of being with me. He held onto it for six years and now he got it out of his system, and I think he will leave me alone.

I hate the fact that my heart pangs when I decide I can't see him again. It should be the obvious choice, but part of me is arguing.

I hurry out of the building and out into the street. This red dress looks ridiculous in day light. The people walking past me are wearing jeans and slacks and normal dresses. It's so obvious that I am wearing the same thing I wore last night, and I am doing the walk of shame.

I keep my eyes low, wishing for the Uber to arrive quickly. Even though I am embarrassed I can't help smiling to myself. I know what it's like to be with a man - and oh my word it is *amazing*. Whether or not I want to, I will fantasize about him for a while.

The driver pulls up next to me and I duck inside.

He grins at me in the rearview mirror. "Did you have a fun night?" He teases.

"I did, thank you very much." I snark back at him.

I click my phone to check my messages, now that I am out of his place, I want to see who was looking for me last night. Hayley, wondering why I am so quiet - and an email from the HR department at my new job. I click on it, eager to read it but my phone battery dies before it opens.

Dammit.

Excitement rushes through me and causes butterflies to dance around in my stomach. My new job is starting next week - it's so close. That's all I need to think about. That's all that matters.

This whole thing with Tuomo should be over now that he got what he wanted, and I can carry on with my life.

The Uber driver stops outside my apartment.

"Thank you." I say, climbing out, carrying my high heels in my hands. I rush upstairs. I want to plug my phone in, get out of this dress and have a shower.

Then I can sit down and read the email from the law firm.

Lifting my legs up and tucking them beneath me I snuggle into my little one-seater chair with a cup of tea. With excitement I open the email and start reading it.

> *Nerissa,*
> *We are excited to have you starting with us next week –*

The email details my working hours, who I should report to when I arrive and a few of the things I can expect to be handling in my first week there.

I read it twice to make sure I don't miss any information. Then I set my phone aside, grinning, and sip my tea, proud of myself.

I've worked so hard to get to this point and I deserve to take a moment and just soak it in. My mom would be proud. I wish she could be here to tell me that herself. But I know what she would say. *Nerissa, you have always been the smartest girl, of course they want you to work there, they are lucky to have you.* I grin, picturing her smile. She would hug me really tightly and I'd lean my head against her chest.

It's hard not to have her around. But at least I know I am doing the best I can.

The next week is a whirl wind. I start this coming Monday, and I have a lot to do before then.

As I expected I don't hear from Tuomo after our very passionate night together. This makes me a little disappointed, but it's for the best. It's what I wanted. Of course, it doesn't stop me from thinking about him. He keeps sneaking into my thoughts, especially at night when it's quiet and I am trying to fall asleep. I tell myself it's ok to fantasize as long as I keep my distance from him. It sucks he ghosted me just like all the other guys, but instead of moping around and feeling rejected I focus on what I need to. Getting ready for my new job. On Friday I have lunch with Hayley, followed by a stressful shopping session while we try to choose a few key items for me to wear to work that are versatile enough for me to wear daily with no one noticing it's the same item. I can't afford to buy a whole new wardrobe. Especially not before I get paid. So, I need to be crafty. I can barely afford the things we find.

Thank goodness Hayley has an eye for fashion and an excellent ability to save money without compromising style.

Late on Friday afternoon I am standing in my little bachelor apartment with the new clothes spread out on my bed. Hayley is a star. She kept it simple and elegant. And every item she chose matches with the other items to create several unique looks.

That's it.

I'm ready.

On Monday morning my new life begins, and everything falls in place for my perfect future.

I clear out a shelf in my closet that will now only be reserved for work clothes.

By the time I am done resorting my closet it's late and I'm ready to crawl into bed.

My phone chimes and I rush over to it, expecting Hayley to be checking in with me.

My heart jumps into my throat when I see Tuomo's name on the screen.

My hand shakes with nervous excitement.

I didn't realize how much I wanted to hear from him until this exact moment.

I open the message and read it.

> Tuomo: Hello, beautiful girl. I've been thinking about you the entire week. All I wanted to say was good luck. You are going to be brilliant.

A massive smile spreads across my face. The message is sweet and thoughtful.

Then I realize what is happening, and I put my phone down.

No, we don't smile at messages from Tuomo Vece. We ignore them. Because he is not good for us.

I sigh, kicking my shoes off to get into my pajamas. His message is still on my mind when I climb into bed. I shouldn't be rude. I should at least say thank you.

Picking up my phone I tire a quick response.

> Me: Thanks. I'm really excited. I hope you have been well.

There. Done.

I shove my phone under my pillow. It chimes again and I hesitate. It's him, but it if read it I will want to reply again.

No. I need to put a stop to this before it gets out of hand.

But as I fall asleep, I picture him - his gorgeous muscular body pinning me down and that devilish smile of his.

CHAPTER SEVENTEEN
Tuomo

Day after day I follow her.

The night I spent with her has only strengthened my love.

The experience of having her in my arms has made it even clearer to me we are meant to be together. It has given me the patience to trust the process of my plan.

So, I've been quiet, and I've been watching her.

I knew she wouldn't reach out to me, it's not a surprise, but it is annoying. Perhaps I had some hope that she would. But she will soon. She will when she finds out she is pregnant with my baby.

At night I read through her messages and call logs and browse her emails.

Installing a watcher app on her phone was easy. Everything with her is easy because she is so innocent she doesn't know what this world is really about. And she never has to find out. I can protect her from everything and everyone. I am the one who will keep her safe and take care of her.

Lying in bed after following Nerissa and her friend Hayley around the mall for a few hours, I read through the welcome email that the company she is going to work at sent her. I'm not happy about this.

If she really likes the job, she might decide to stay quiet about the baby, or worse, to choose not to have it. I can't risk that.

Also, I need her in a bad place. I need her to need me. If she loses this job, it will break her heart, and that means that I can be there to pick her up again and be her hero.

It just so happens that my family has made use of several law firms in the city. In fact, we have a retainer with this one and all I have to do is make a call.

Dialing the number of our lawyer in that office I press the phone against my ear.

"Mr. Vece. When you call me on a Friday night, It must be urgent. What can I do for you?"

"Hi, David. I need a favor. It's about a woman your company has recently hired. She starts on Monday."

"Alright? What about the girl?" he asks, curious.

"She is important to me, and I don't want her to work at your firm. Or anywhere for that matter. I need you to cancel her contract."

"Oh." He says in shock. "We are very careful about who we choose to work for us. She must have impressed the boss if she got hired. Is there no way we can—"

"No. Make it happen."

He sighs. "Not a problem. I will make sure she is let down gently. Is there anything else I can do for you?"

"Thanks David, that will be all." I hang up the phone and nod to myself.

It's as easy as that.

The power of my name and the money in my bank means I can do and have anything I want.

Just to be sure, I send out an email to the other law firms I work with and inform them I would prefer them not to hire Nerissa. I don't even have to say why, my email alone is enough to stop the process just in case she applies at the other firms in the city.

I feel a touch of guilt for doing this to her, but really, it's not about her - it's about us and our future. It's for the best and she will soon come to realize that.

She is going to learn to trust that I know better. That I know what she needs.

Once I have sorted out the minor issue of her new job, I decide to message her. Because I want to be fresh in her mind when things fall apart. I will step in at the perfect time and offer her a shoulder to lean on.

> Me: Hello, beautiful girl. I've been thinking about you the entire week. You've been getting ready to start your new job, so I wanted you to focus on that. All I wanted to say was good luck. You are going to be brilliant.

I stare at the screen, knowing she is reading it. Her status says she is online.

There is a long pause, and she says nothing in return. Annoyances patterns along the edges of my thoughts. Is she ignoring me? Who the fuck does she think she is?

She types and I shake my head. Calm down, Tuomo. Patience, remember.

> Nerissa: Thanks. I'm really excited. I hope you have been well.

> Me: On Monday after work, I'd like to take you for a celebratory dinner. Or just a drink. Whatever you prefer. What time can I fetch you?

I wait, but she doesn't come online again. My jaw clenches as I try to stop myself from sending her a second message demanding that she reply to me. I place my phone onto my bedside table. It's fine.

She will be crawling back to me soon. Pregnant with my child and begging me to be with her.

Frustration makes it hard to fall asleep.

Annoyance about her lack of response and the constant thoughts I have about how incredible she felt against my body. I want her again. I want her every single night.

I toss and turn for an hour before I drift to sleep.

Saturday morning arrives and I wake up groaning and moody because I have a family lunch this afternoon. I can think of nothing worse than wasting a Saturday with my father. My brothers are annoying, but I can still handle them. My father is just unpleasant through and through. He is a horrible person to be around and all I do when I'm there is sit in silence, waiting for it to be over.

But I have no choice.

So, at twelve o'clock I walk into my father's house with a smile on my face and a bottle of wine in my hand.

"Hello. Hello." I say, trying to sound cheerful.

"Hey bro. There are cold beers in the fridge." Masaccio says, gesturing towards the kitchen as he walks past me out onto the patio.

"Grab one for me." Rufino shouts from outside on the patio.

I walk into the kitchen and find my sister, Dalila, making a salad.

"Hi, Tuo. There are cold beers in the fridge."

"Hi, D. Where's your man?" I ask, opening the fridge door and scanning the shelves.

"Nevio is out on the patio I think - getting the coals going for the meat. We're having steak."

"Sounds amazing. I'll grab a few beers and go check on them out there."

"Please make sure they don't burn the food this time." She calls out to me as I leave the kitchen with a few beers in my hand.

I roll my eyes. Since when does anyone care what I have to say about the food. If she wants the steak done a certain way, she can come out here and argue with them herself. I prefer to stay out of it all as much as possible.

Around the barbecue my brothers and Nevio are chatting and laughing at each other's stories. They all seem to be relaxed and enjoying themselves. Maybe it's just me, but I never belong here.

"Who wants a beer?" I ask, walking towards them, holding the beers up in the air.

"Me, thanks man." Nevio says as he closes the grill and nods with satisfaction at whatever he has done inside there.

Celso slaps me on the back. "Late as usual." He taunts.

I ignore him, sipping my beer and standing amongst them, listening to their ongoing conversations about business, cars, and a new house Masaccio is thinking about buying.

It's all boring to me.

I nod, and make a random comment here and there, but in reality, my mind is on Nerissa.

I wonder how long it will take before she finds out she isn't starting her job anymore. Will she already have been contacted this morning or will they wait until Monday?

I wonder how long it will be before she shows symptoms of being pregnant.

I might have to have a plan in place to get that information out of her in case she finds out and tries to keep it from me.

I'll figure it out as I go.

She will tell Hayley, and I'll see the messages on her phone.

"Tuomo." Rufino says, throwing a beer cap at me to get my attention.

"What?"

"How do you want your steak done?"

"Medium rare."

Masaccio and his wife are sitting on the outdoor sofas. He has his arm wrapped around her waist and she's leaning into his neck, giggling and nuzzling against him. I watch with morbid fascination wondering how someone like Masaccio found love before me. He is the last person on the planet I would have expected to get married.

"Dad's home." Dalila calls out to us from inside.

She walks onto the patio, straight towards Nevio who wraps his arms around her and kisses her. "Are you burning the steak?" She asks him with her eyes narrowed.

"What? Never." He replies.

She stands on her tiptoes and kisses him again. "If you do, you'll be in trouble."

"I enjoy being in trouble with you." He laughs.

I roll my eyes and turn my back to them.

My father strides into the gathering and my body goes stiff.

Fuck. I just want to leave. I don't care about any of this.

I want to be with Nerissa.

CHAPTER EIGHTEEN
Nerissa

Reading the email again my eyes well with tears. I blink them away in disbelief and read it once more. It can't be. This can't be happening. Is this some kind of sick joke?

It's Sunday morning and the last thing I expected when I opened my emails was to find a very curt and formal message from the law firm notifying me I am fired before I even started.

"Due to unforeseen circumstances—" I huff, my throat is tight as a big lump sits there and I can no longer hold back the tears. "We have decided to go in a different direction." I slam the laptop closed. I can't read another word.

I cry like a child who has been told they can't get a puppy when it's all they have been dreaming of. I can't stop crying so I push my laptop away from myself and flop face down onto my bed, burying my face into my pillow so that my neighbors don't hear my heavy sobs through the thin walls.

The universe must hate me to taunt me with something so amazing and then snatch it away.

Their email doesn't even make sense. None of this makes sense. It was all set in stone. I thought it was a done deal.

I shake my head, nuzzling my face harder against the pillow as tears continue to soak into the fabric.

I cry for over an hour and then pass out from exhaustion. When I wake up, just for a moment, I pretend it was a nightmare. But my swollen, burning eyes are all the proof I need. I sit up, sighing and wondering what to do with myself. I'm numb and empty. It's as if my future has been ripped out from beneath my feet.

Well, there is no point in lying around in bed all day feeling sorry for myself. I should message Hayley and ask her to go for coffee with me.

I pick up my phone and stare at it.

I'm too embarrassed to tell her what's happened. I feel like such a failure.

After I've had a cup of tea, I'll figure out what to do.

Focusing on each small step in making the tea I lose myself in the task and for a few minutes I feel a little lighter.

I carry the tea to the chair and sit looking out of the small window to the street down below where people are going about their day as though it was the most normal Sunday in the world.

I should get out there and go for a walk or something. Staying inside here is only going to make me feel worse. But the thought of getting dressed and doing something so normal makes me cry again.

My phone chimes and I sigh. I guess I was going to face Hayley at some point.

But the message is from Tuomo.

> Tuomo: Hi, little bird. Good luck for tomorrow. I'll see you after for the celebrations?

I chew at my lip, knowing I'm playing with fire.

> Me: There won't be any celebrations. More like drowning my sorrows.

> Tuomo: Why? What's going on?

> Me: They went in another direction. I don't have a job anymore. I'm kind of heartbroken about it.

> Tuomo: I'm coming to fetch you right now. We can have ice-cream on the beach, and you can forget those assholes who don't deserve you.

I should say no. I should call Hayley instead. But somehow, I don't care if I'm making a mistake or not.

> Me: I'll get ready.

I've been thinking about this guy every day since I snuck out of his room. When I see his name on my phone, it makes my heartbeat so fast, I get dizzy. And right now, I deserve a little distraction from this horrible day.

Rushing around my apartment I pull on a pair of skinny high wasted jeans and a crop top along with my colorful sneakers. Grabbing a jacket, I shove my phone into the pocket and then rush out of the door. The excitement and thrill of seeing Tuomo again has made me forget about that stupid email. It's exactly what I needed.

As I walk out onto the street outside my apartment Tuomo pulls up. He climbs out of the car and walks around to my side to open the door. When I step close to climb inside, he grabs me and kisses me. I giggle and blush. His smile is full of mischief and his eyes are soothing to me.

He drives us through the city with the windows down and the music turned up loud. His hand is on my thigh, and it's so normal - it feels fantastic. It's a beautiful day and the hot summery air pushes into the car making my skin glow. I float my hand out of the window, dancing it on the breeze and letting my thoughts slip away in the wind.

Tuomo parks along the promenade. A long strip of walkway that wraps around the edge of the ocean separating the city from the water. We climb out and as soon as he is next to me, he slips his hand into mine.

We get ice cream in a waffle cone with a chocolate hidden inside. We walk along the edge of the ocean, listening to the waves and laughing about people, making up stories about what they might be talking about and who they are.

Tuomo makes me laugh with his imaginative thoughts and the characters he creates.

I'm having so much fun it scares me.

I haven't laughed this much in ages. I haven't felt this good around someone - ever.

"Will you let me take you on another date?" he asks as we stand leaning against the railing near the edge of the promenade. High tide waves are crashing against the wall beneath us and the spray is shooting up in a salty mist and covering my skin. I love the smell of the ocean.

He turns towards me, leaning his hip against the railing. "Little bird?" he says, forcing my attention onto him so that I have to answer his question.

I sigh and squeeze my eyes tight for a second, then nod. "Yes." I blurt out. Surprising myself because I was dead set on not seeing him again.

Today was - it was a decision made in a moment of weakness. I was down, and I agreed to see him. But it's been too much fun, and I can't be having fun with a guy like Tuomo.

"Yes." He chuckles, grabbing my jaw and pressing his lips against mine.

His tongue tastes of vanilla and chocolate and his lips taste salty from the ocean spray.

He slips his arms around my waist and holds me tight as though I am with him.

I lean into him, standing on my tip toes to deepen the kiss. Flashes of the other night taunt my mind. My heart races.

Why does he feel so right for me?

I push away from him, my hands against his solid chest.

"I - I should get back home."

"Are you sure? We can get a bite to eat if you like?"

"I need to send my resume out to other law firms." I say, hit by the pang of sadness again. I really wanted that job. But if I can't have it, I will keep trying. I'll find something else. There are several law firms in this city, and I will apply to every single one of them if I have to.

"Alright, little bird. I understand. But keep Wednesday night open. I've planned something very special for us. A night you always remember." He kisses me again, a soft, tender kiss. Then he takes my hand, and we walk back towards his car.

My thoughts are full of warnings, red-flags, and concern about how quickly I am becoming entangled with him. When my head is cleared, I'll cancel our date. Over text it will be easier than face-to-face. When he looks at me with those dark eyes, I can't seem to say no to him.

I'll pull myself together, and tomorrow, I'll send him a really polite cancellation.

Monday morning rushes by so fast I can't believe it when I look at the time and see it's three o'clock. I haven't eaten yet, I haven't checked my phone in hours - but I have sent my resume out to five law firms with a great covering letter tailored to each one depending on the position I am applying for.

It will take a few days, even a week, for them to get back to me - but it's done, and I'm optimistic about it.

I'm too tired to think, I still need to message Tuomo and cancel our date, but I am going to leave it till tomorrow. He's going to be annoyed if I do it now, or wait. But at least tomorrow I'll be able to deal with it better.

I stand up and stretch my arms above my head. Sitting for so long is bad for me. My body aches. I should grab my yoga mat and go down to the park for a bit. That will help me clear my head.

My laptop chimes, indicating I have received an email.

I open it, expecting a generic 'thank you for your email, we will get back to you' vibe. But as I scan it flop back down into the chair.

It's a decline.

Straight away.

How could they even have had time to go through my information? Did they read the covering letter? Another email comes in - another decline. My heart sinks.

What is going on?

By Tuesday morning every single application has been declined and none of them have given me a logical reason. I feel like my life is falling apart and I don't even understand why. What did I do wrong?

When Tuomo messages me to confirm our date, I reply yes.

I need the distraction.

CHAPTER NINETEEN
Tuomo

Nerissa steps onto my yacht and her pretty floral blue dress floats up in the cool afternoon breeze. I told her to wear flat shoes, and she has her colorful sneakers on with the short flowing dress and I can't stop staring at.

"I can't believe you are taking me on a yacht." She says.

"And the chef is making an incredible salmon dish for dinner. You are going to love it."

She grins, turning her back to me as she walks further onto the deck.

I step behind her, wrapping my arm around her stomach and kissing her neck.

"Shall we have cocktails and lie in the sun?"

"Oh, I didn't bring my swim suit."

"I bought a few for you, in case you didn't bring one. I think I got the size right, and I chose a few different colors - although I can guess which one you'll like best."

She laughs. "How would you know which one I'd like best?"

"Because I know everything about you. And whatever I don't know - I want to learn."

I lead her below deck to the bedroom where I've already put the bikinis out for her to choose. She doesn't need to know right now, but I've also packed fresh clothes for her tomorrow as the yacht won't be returning to the dock until the morning. She is spending the night with me tonight - and I've made it impossible for her to sneak away from me before I wake up this time. There's no running away out at sea.

"Alright. I know which one I like. Before I pick it up, why don't you tell me which one you *think* I was going to choose." She says her hands on her hips.

"A test. This should be fun." I grin as I walk straight over to the mint green one in a ruffled fabric. I pick it up and hand it to her. She frowns, pouting her lip out.

"But how did you know?"

I can't tell her she shared a screenshot of this exact bikini with Hayley captioned 'when I'm rich I'll laze about on my yacht wearing this'.

"I think it suites you the best. The color will be amazing on your skin."

She is still frowning, but she shrugs and holds the bikini against her chest. "Where can I change?"

"In here. I'll wait for you up on the deck. There is a summer robe hanging on the back of the door for you as well.

"Thank you, Tuomo. I didn't expect all of this."

I hold her face and kiss the top of her forehead. "Hurry, I want to see you in that." I wink.

A glint of mischief flashes in her eyes before I turn and leave the room.

I am up on the deck with virgin Pino coladas ready and waiting when she steps into view.

My heart slamming against my rib cage.

The sheer black lace cover-up and the mint bikini are incredible on her. She looks like she has stepped off a runway. The smile on her face is one full of confidence and I love to see her this way.

She walks up to me with her hips swaying and my eyes can't stop soaking her in.

"I did not expect it to look that good." I smirk.

Nerissa lets me rub tanning oil on her skin and I take my time, running my hands over every inch of her, fighting the urge to slip my fingers beneath the bikini and make her moan. When I'm done and she turns to face me again and I have to sit in a way that hides my hard-on.

I sip my drink and wait for my cock to settle before I lie back on the sun lounger.

She gets comfortable next to me, lying close to me and making me smile.

The staff are on form and as soon as our drinks finish, they have another one ready.

They've been informed I don't want her drinking alcohol. All the cocktails are virgin. If she is pregnant, I don't want to take any risks.

Nerissa is staring out towards the ocean, enjoying the wide expanse of nothing and the bright blue sky, but I am looking at her. I can't fathom how one person can be this perfect.

She can tell my eyes are on her and turns towards me. "This is so beautiful. I've never been this far out at sea before."

"There are so many things I want to show you, Nerissa. I can take you all over the world. We can travel together, have incredible adventures." I stop myself, worried that I am being too intense again.

She scrunches her nose, looking cute. "I can't afford to travel, Tuomo. And I'm struggling to find a job. Everyone keeps turning me down."

I reach out and brush the pad of my thumb over the very smooth and soft skin of her cheek. "With me you will never need to work a day in your life. You will have everything your heart desires, even the things you haven't imagined yet."

She blushes and looks away from me, back out towards the ocean.

"I don't think life is a fairytale." She says with a touch of melancholy. "We have to work for things, or we don't appreciate them."

I sit up a little, propping myself onto my elbow and leaning over her.

"I never said it was. I haven't had a fairytale life. It's far from perfect. But you make me believe in things that seem impossible. With you, I think love and true happiness exist. Life *can be* a fairy tale if you let me make it one."

Her eyes pierce into mine, the sun turning them golden as she stares up at me. She looks at me for a long time saying nothing. She hasn't said no. She hasn't disagreed with me. I think she is beginning to believe the same things I believe. That we are supposed to be together.

I lean further over her, pressing my lips against hers and lowering my body onto hers. Her skin is hot from the sun, glistening with oil.

My hands explore the smooth curves of her body, and my cock grows hard against her.

She spreads her legs open for me and I rock myself against her pussy.

Tugging at the string of her bikini I pull it free from her body and toss it to the side. She looks around.

"Don't worry. No one will bother us." I chuckle, pull her face back towards me and kissing her fiercely. I sit up, tugging her bikini bottom off, rubbing my hand up the inside of her thighs.

The sun bakes down on our naked bodies as we explore each other in the open, salty air.

I pull her legs apart and nuzzle my mouth against her soft pink pussy. She moans and rocks her hips against my face, her fingers knot in my hair. I dip my tongue deep inside her, tasting her sweetness and licking her warmth.

She moves against me while I fuck her with my mouth.

I want to give her everything. I have to make it clear to her I am all she will ever need in this world. Nothing and no one else matters but us. If we have each other, we can do anything.

She moans, no longer caring if anyone hears her, lost in the pleasure I am giving her.

Her legs shake, wrapped around my shoulders and I move my tongue faster over her clit, pushing my fingers inside her.

When she comes, it makes me as hard as a rock.

I get up, positioning myself in front of her and then with a dark smile I thrust my cock inside her.

She cries out in fright and pleasure gripping the edge of the sun lounger.

Every time I push into her, I watch her breasts bounce. The sun is setting across the ocean and a bright orange and pink sky is reflecting in her eyes. She bites her lips as she stares at me, breathless and beautiful, taking my entire cock inside her and loving every inch.

"Your pussy was made for me, little bird." I growl, grabbing her hips and pulling her down onto me as I thrust in again. I want to be deeper. I want to possess her.

I fuck her hard until her pussy tightens over me, and she orgasms again. I explode inside her at the same time. Knowing she is already carrying my baby, but happy to keep trying just in case she isn't.

When we are done, the sun is already so low, dipping right into the ocean, that is sky is growing dark. It looks beautiful around us as we pull our swimwear back on and Nerissa grabs the black lace gown, wrapping it over her shoulders.

I pull her close. "It's getting a little colder out here. I have some warm clothes for you in the cabin - then we can sit up on the top deck and enjoy our dinner, if you're hungry?"

"That sounds perfect." She says, letting me lead her back into the cabin.

CHAPTER TWENTY
Nerissa

Waking up on a yacht is an unfamiliar experience for me. The ocean is rocking us and while some people find it horrible, I find it really soothing.

I slept so deeply and don't even remember dreaming. Of course, that could have been because Tuomo exhausted me before he wrapped his arms around me and covered me in the blanket. I was too tired to think, and I fell asleep almost instantly.

He is already awake and watching me when I blink my eyes open.

"Hi, beautiful." He says in a deep, husky morning voice.

"Morning." I say, self-consciously brushing my hand across my face and wondering how bad I look. My make up must be smudged across my eyes and my hair will be full of knots and standing up in all directions. But Tuomo is still looking at me as though I am the most gorgeous girl on the planet.

"I've messaged the chef and told him he can prepare breakfast." He says, leaning down and kissing me.

Dammit.

I can't believe this happened again.

I am so bad at staying away from him and even worse at not ending up in his bed.

I don't know what it is about him, but I lose all control and become weak when I'm near him. He makes me feel so safe and so comfortable that I seem to stop using my brain all together.

After a lazy, slow breakfast the yacht takes us back to shore and Tuomo drops me at home.

As soon as I am alone, the pang of worry and guilt gets stronger.

I am playing dangerous games and I'm going to end up really hurt or in some kind of trouble.

But when I'm with Tuomo, he's the perfect guy, and he makes *me* feel amazing. He isn't the perfect guy though. He's dangerous. He's not someone you mess with and not someone I should be falling for.

But that's ridiculous. I'm not falling for him.

I'm just - enjoying a little fun.

My stomach churns as I climb the stairs up to my apartment.

I push the door open and walk inside.

I remember the night of my birthday. How terrified I was when he pinned me against the bed, how I thought he was here to kill me. It seems like a distant nightmare now. As though I imagined it. Or, like it happened, but I made it seem worse in my mind than it really was.

No. I shake my head, sitting down on the edge of my bed and fidgeting my hands in my lap. I didn't imagine it. Tuomo has that side to him. It could come out at any moment, and I should never ever forget about it - even when he seems so perfect.

He isn't.

My phone chimes and I slide the screen to open the message.

> Tuomo: I miss you already. I can't wait to see you again. Can I fetch you tomorrow for a picnic in the park?

Smiling at his message.

Shit.

This is so bad.

I think I need to spend some time with other friends. I should call Hayley. She doesn't even know I haven't started work yet, or that I got declined at all the other jobs, because I've ignored her last few messages, just replying *sorry, I'm really busy, will chat soon*. And I only wrote that because if I said nothing at all she would come and bash my door down because she'd think I'd died alone on the floor of my apartment.

It's not fair of me to keep all of this from her. She's been there for me through everything for the past few years. We are really close.

I should tell her what's going on.

"What am I doing?" I huff, flopping backwards onto my bed.

I sit up again, my head is too busy, and I need to clear it. I never got around to doing yoga in the park. I stand up and wiggle out of the clothes I am wearing and search my closet for my gym tights and crop top. Dressed, I grab my yoga mat and a bottle of water. Purposefully leaving my phone behind because I need space to think and I can't do that if Tuomo keeps messaging me, I leave the apartment and start walking towards the park.

It's another beautiful day, even though the sun is not as bright as it was yesterday, the soft layer of gray clouds is peaceful and eases the heat away a bit.

I love summer, but what I really love is over Christmas when it snows. I've always wanted to cuddle someone special as we sat by a massive fireplace and sipped hot chocolate together.

I also want to do other, sexier things in front of a fireplace. I grin to myself, picture Tuomo and the magical things he did with his mouth last night.

Then I roll my eyes and get annoyed with myself and the woman walking towards me throws me a weird look. She thought I was rolling my eyes at her. I should really pay attention to what my face is doing. It's hard to hide your emotions when you paint them all over your face.

I smile at her, but it's too late. She's already offended. She snubs her nose at me and walks faster, passing me with a huff.

The rest of the walk to the park I ignore my thoughts and pay attention to the here and now. Live in the moment. It's the best way to ease anxiety or worry that's bothering you.

I watch the people and listen to all the sounds of the city.

There are a couple of people doing yoga in the park already. It's popular here, near the pond. Even with kids running back and forth, screaming, and laughing, it's easy to relax and zone out.

However, every single position I get into makes me think of Tuomo.

I keep picturing him folding me this way and that way and bending me over just like this. It's driving me crazy and making me so horny I can't focus on my breathing.

I push through the entire sequence which lasts forty-five minutes, but it's messy and my breathing is off, and it makes me more flustered than anything else.

At the end of it I just lie on my back staring at the sky and the tops of the trees moving in the wind.

I'm hopeless.

The next day Tuomo takes me out again.

And then day after that.

And every day that I spend with him makes it easier to forget the dangers and pretend that he is the perfect man for me.

One night, walking along the waterfront with the city lights shining in across the water he takes my hand and stops me. I turn to face him, and he pulls me close to his chest, wrapping his arms around me.

"Little bird." His deep voice rumbles against my chest. I stare up into his dark chocolate eyes.

"Mm?" I say, looking at his lips, wanting to kiss him again.

"I want you to know how much you mean to me. The time we spend together - it's not just casual fun to me. It's really special. I appreciate every moment with you."

I shift nervously against him.

I love it when he speaks like this. I love hearing his heart and he seems to wear it on his sleeve when he is around me. It's so mature that he can speak about his emotions openly.

But it makes me nervous too because I am scared to tell him how I feel.

I am scared to admit to myself how I've fallen for him.

"You don't have to say anything, little bird." He smiles. "You don't have to be ready for anything. I just want you to know how special you are."

I shake my head, lowering my eyes because I'm nervous.

"You are really special to me too, Tuomo." I whisper.

He puts his finger beneath my chin and lifts my face up towards his.

"I didn't hear you." His voice is mesmerizing.

"You are really special to me." I repeat, staring right into his eyes, drowning in them, being pulled so deep into him I don't know if I will ever be able to make my way out again.

He leans forward and presses his lips against mine.

His tongue slips into my mouth as we kiss.

I can't help it. No matter what I do to stop it from happening my heart is making its own choices about him.

And now I accept the truth.

I'm, stupidly, falling for him.

CHAPTER TWENTY-ONE
Tuomo

"Another meeting?" I pace in agitation up and down my living room. "We just had a meeting."

Rufino is on the other side of the phone and he's telling me I have to be at my father's mansion just after breakfast.

"This meeting is important, Tuomo. What the fuck is going on with you? Why can't you just do as you're told and not argue about everything?" Rufino sounds exhausted. I run my fingers through my hair and stop pacing.

"Are you ok?" I ask, wondering why he doesn't sound like himself.

"Oh - you fucking care, do you? Just be at the house at eleven."

"Fine. I'll be there. I was just—" He hung up on me. Fucking asshole always hangs up on me. I wouldn't be bothered if I saw none of my brothers again - or my father. Especially my father.

Being a part of this family infuriates me.

I want freedom from them. I want them to leave me alone so that I can live my life - with Nerissa.

But, like the dutiful son I have to be, I head over to my father's place at eleven.

Walking into the living room I can tell that something is off. My brothers, Masaccio, Rufino, and Celso are all seated already, and my father is standing behind his chair with his hands resting on the back of it. They are all looking at me. Everyone is silent, and their eyes are so locked onto my that I can feel the heat of their stares. No one looks comfortable, and that makes me very uncomfortable as well.

"What's going on?" I ask, walking closer. "Has something happened? Where's Dalila?" My heart pains when I realize she's not here and I assume that something must have happened to her.

No one answers me. They just keep looking at me with their stupid, silent faces. "Where the fuck is Dalila?" I repeat.

"Sit down, Tuomo." My father's deep voice commands.

My heart is beating too fast now. Deep concern for my sister's well-being is flooding my senses and causing anxiety to boil through me.

I watch them as I take a seat, the furthest one away from their circle of staring faces. I sit on the edge of the seat with my elbows resting on my knees as I lean forward. Waiting. Full of anticipation.

My father takes a deep breath.

"Your sister is at home. She's fine. This isn't about her."

I press my hand against my chest, relief washing through me, but the tension remains. If it's not about her, what is it about?

Pressing my lips together I force myself to match their silence. Whatever game they are playing - I can do the same.

My father turns towards me. His steel-gray eyes are dark, like a thunder cloud is brewing just beneath the surface of his gaze.

"Tuomo, where have you been?" he asks.

I shake my head. "What do you mean?"

"What have you been up to? Because you haven't been doing your fucking job - that's for sure."

Mas clears his throat and my father glances towards him. He pulls his mouth tight, straighten his back as he rolls his shoulders. "What I mean is." He takes a breath. "We need to know what is going on with you because we've all noticed your absence."

I stand up, shocked to my core. "Is this a fucking intervention?" I snarl. "What? I'm not allowed to have a life? I have to report every second of every day to you?"

Mas raises his hand in a gesture of peace. "It's not like that, Tuo. We are worried about you. You've been distant and some things that are your duty -

you've been neglecting things - we just want to know if you are alright."

My father shakes his head. "Stop pandering to him. He's a grown man. He fucked up, and he has to answer for it."

"How did I fuck up?" I ask.

"The shipment that was supposed to go out on Thursday morning. The one you were supposed to oversee." Rufino says, lifting one corner of his mouth and raising his brows towards me. "And bro, it's not the first thing you've failed to arrive for. Stock-take on the weekend. The delivery to the new client who came to the city to meet us face-to-face. Do you want me to go on?"

I shake my head. Rufino said enough.

So, that is what this is about.

I glance down, frowning, trying to figure out how I forgot those appointments. I check my calendar daily. I'm never negligent with my work - so how did this happen?

"Well?" my father demands. "What the hell is going on with you?"

Mas sighs. "Are you ok, Tuomo? Is something going on that you need our help with?"

"No, nothing is going on. I'm fine. I don't know how I missed that - it won't happen again." I stand up. "Are we done here?"

My father sneers. "For fuck's sake." He spits his words.

"Tuo—" Rufino says.

Celso hasn't spoken a word. He's barely looked at me.

"Are we done here? I get it. I fucked up. I said it won't happen again."

"Ye. Ye, we're done." Mas sighs, waving his hand in the air to dismiss me.

My father turns and walks from the room.

That was my one chance with him and I'm lucky he gave me that. He won't be lenient about my mistakes again. Next time I'll probably get punched in the head or some other form of punishment at his hand.

I turn towards the front door and march out of there as fast as I can.

I can't believe that just happened.

I get defensive and embarrassed at the same time.

I didn't realize I was neglecting my duties. But I'm also at a point where I don't think I should have so much pressure on me. I want to live my life and only worry about my business. Not theirs.

I climb into my car and slam the door, revving the engine to life. A knock on my window makes me jump. Rufino is standing there, looking down at me.

I open the window, staring forward. "What?"

"Dude, what is going on man? We're here for you. Dad has weird ways of showing it - but underneath it all we are just worried about you."

"Dad isn't worried about anything but his empire and his cash-flow."

I shove the gear shift into reverse and wheel spin, forcing Rufino to jump out of the way. He swears at me as I drive off.

My heart is racing when I hit the open road and speed forward.

Fuck all of them.

I don't need them.

The only person I need in this world is Nerissa. She is my everything. She is my life.

My fists clench the steering wheel, rubbing back and forth. Thoughts of her flooding mind and constrict my heart.

I can't explain how or why but when I think about her, it's different.

That possessive streak is still very much there - she *is* mine. She belongs to me. But now there is something else too. A fear.

I never want to lose her. The fear of that thought sits tight in my chest. Losing something has never struck fear into my heart until now.

I take a deep breath, trying to process this new emotion.

She means everything to me. When I picture her smile, it makes me smile.

I want not only to possess her I want to make her happy. I want to create a beautiful life for her.

I've never been *gentle* towards someone before. Tenderness is not a reaction I'm used to. But with

Nerissa that is what I have. She slows my mind, softens me, makes me want to wrap my arms around her and hold her until the end of time.

Cars rush past me. This is ridiculous. What the hell is going on with me? I'm just annoyed by the intervention. That's all.

I want to go to Nerissa. But I won't. I have to prove to myself that she doesn't control me. I am the only person who is in control here.

I need to get home and clear my head.

CHAPTER TWENTY-TWO
Nerissa

Sitting at the small wooden bar chair at my kitchen counter with a bowl of cold noodles in front of me I have been ignoring for twenty minutes, I read the message Hayley sent me again. It worries me because she's right. But I also don't really want to admit she's right because that is a whole different can of worms I don't want to open.

> Hayley: What is going on with you? You don't reply to my messages. I don't even see you anymore. It's like you fell off the planet. Did I offend you or do you not want to be friends with me anymore? Please talk to me.

I have fallen off the planet. The only person I ever spend time with is Tuomo. And I have been avoiding her messages because I don't know how to explain that to her. Because I know what I'm doing is wrong. I shouldn't be with him. But that doesn't mean I should just ditch my best friend and not tell her about everything.

I sigh, my fingers hovering over the keyboard. I don't know what to say.

It's too much to explain over one message and *I* can't understand what's going on so how can I tell her?

If I look at my behavior over the past while, it has become erratic and irresponsible. I'm not focused on the right things anymore.

Have to reply to her though. I can't just leave this.

She thinks I'm mad at her. I feel horrible about that.

I type, delete it, and start again.

Why is this so difficult?

> Me: Hi babe, I'm really sorry I've been so distant. The truth is I ended up not getting that job - the one I was meant to start last Monday, and it messed with my head a lot. I've just been lying low and trying to figure my life out. I'm not mad at you at all and it means a lot to me you have been messaging. I'm an asshole for not replying. I love you lots, and we must get together soon.

I hit send and my stomach churns. I'm a shit friend.

Putting my phone face down on the counter because I can't even bear to look at my reflection in the dark screen, I pull the bowl of noodles back towards myself and push the fork into them, swooshing them back and forth. I can't keep doing this.

I need to get my life together.

Being with Tuomo is going to get me nowhere. He is distracting me from what's important. And I'll fall for him and then boom - he will get bored with me and ditch me like a ton of bricks. I deserve more.

I should know better, but apparently, I've lost all sense of responsibility and reason.

Rolling my eyes at myself I sigh and force a forkful of noodles into my mouth. I can't afford to waste food.

I'm jobless, soon to be homeless if I don't get my ass into gear.

I pull a face as I chew, because the noodles are pretty gross cold, I decide to make a point of saying *no* when Tuomo asks me out the next time. I have to set up some healthy boundaries. My life is busy falling apart and all I seem to be focused on is how good he makes me feel. But that's temporary. My career, and future, and goals are so much more important.

I finish my noodles and rinse the bowl, setting it upside down in the drying rack.

It's almost three in the afternoon and I should get online and do some job hunting. I feel so unmotivated it's scary.

But I have to.

I turn from the kitchen sink and my apartment door flies open.

I scream in fright, not knowing what the hell is going on.

Hayley bursts inside like a tornado. She is scowling, but also relieved - and it confuses me.

"Oh good. You're alive. Are you on drugs? Did you become an alcoholic or something? What the hell, Nerissa. You can't just ignore me and then send me a message like that." She is talking fast and as she waves her phone at me.

"Hayley, oh my word you gave me a heart attack."

"And what do you think you've done to me with all the ignoring and bullshit? You didn't start working? I thought you've been too busy to reply?"

Shit.

I told her that.

I bite my bottom lip and stare at her, wondering how to explain the mess I'm in.

Her eyes soften when she sees my expression and the tension in my stance.

"It's three o'clock and you're still in your pajamas." She sighs. "Oh man. You really need to tell me what's going on." She walks over to me and pulls me into a tight hug. I lean against her, not realizing how badly I needed this.

When she steps back, she takes my hand and leads me to the bed, forcing me to sit down. Then she goes to the kitchen and grabs two wine glasses, carrying them back to where I'm sitting.

She sighs as she drags the armchair right next to the bed and sits down in it, kicking her shoes off and stretching her legs out onto the bed.

"You may as well get comfortable, girl, because I'm not going anywhere until you tell me what is going on." She says, pouring us each a glass of wine.

I lean forward and take the glass of wine from her.

"It's kind of complicated." I say, swirling the dry white in the glass and watching it splash up against the edges.

"I think you'll find, when you talk, that it's not as complicated as you think."

My voice quakes as I unload my worries onto her, recounting the disappointment of the job falling through and the constant stream of rejections, each one lacking a legitimate reason. A deep sense of fear for what lies ahead engulfs me, leaving me perplexed and unable to make sense of it all.

She listens, topping up the wine glass as we chat. But in all honesty, I am struggling to drink it. I've barely had half a glass, and it's not sitting well with me today. Maybe I'm just too tired. I put the wine glass down on my bedside table.

When I'm done talking, she pulls her mouth into a sarcastic smile. "Ok, but what are you hiding?"

"Huh?"

"So, the job fell through. Ok. That's horrible. But where have you been? What have you been doing?"

Dammit, how does she know me so well?

I glance towards my window, wondering if he's out there right now. I always have this feeling that he's there, just watching. I push the thought aside and turn my attention back onto Hayley.

"I met a guy." I say, sighing, accepting that she won't stop until she finds out the truth.

"A guy? Are you serious? How, where, when?"

"It's someone I used to know before I met you. Someone from my past." I shrug.

"Girl - I can't believe you kept this from me. So, is it serious, are you falling in love, who is he, what's his name?" the questions rush out of her mouth like a freight train.

I chuckle. "Calm down. Jeez."

"Don't tell me to calm down. I want to know everything."

I sigh, getting up to pour myself some water. When I come back, she has her arms folded across her chest, waiting.

"He's a lot older than me. And he's *gorgeous*." I say, sitting back down on the bed.

"Are you in love, Nerissa? How old? Older guys can be so hot." she says with shock.

"It's getting—I—" I sigh. "I am falling for him." I admit, the weight of my words settling in. I can't believe I said it out loud.

I am falling for Tuomo. The exact thing I promised myself not to do.

Hayley finishes the bottle of wine and doesn't seem to pay attention to the fact that I've switched to drinking water. We talk for ages, and she is happy to know what is going on with me. By the time she leaves I'm feeling a lot better. It's funny how a talk with a friend can settle your thoughts and refocus your mind. I really needed that. I'm so glad she forced her way into my day.

I walk over to my curtains to close them so I can get ready for bed, I close them, but tonight I can't shake the sensation that he's watching me.

Putting on my comfortable oversized tee shirt and brushing my teeth I am thinking about him.

It's just because I spoke about him so much tonight. I never told her his name though. Not his full name. She doesn't know he is a Vece. I needed to keep that a secret because I don't want her to lecture me on what a bad idea it is. I already know.

I climb into bed, still confused about what the best way forward is. I am falling for him - and he is bad for me. So, how do I navigate that?

Closing my eyes I snuggle into my bed.

But I can't sleep.

It's driving me crazy.

I get out of bed again and walk to the window, pulling the curtain open.

My heart leaps into my throat.

His car is parked there beneath the streetlamp. He isn't even trying to hide. I should be terrified. I should be offended and creeped out. But I'm not. Somehow his presence out there makes me feel safer.

I walk back to my bed, this time leaving the curtains open. I climb in again and close my eyes.

CHAPTER TWENTY-THREE
Tuomo

I arrive home after the intervention with my family, and I'm restless and angry.

I can't stop pacing around and it's making it worse. I have to do something. I need to get out. Coming home was a bad idea.

I want to stay away from Nerissa, but even after everything that happened today, she is all I can think about. I still don't understand how I was so negligent with my duties. I know better than to piss my father off or draw attention to myself. Nerissa is distracting me from everything. But I love it. I love the way she makes me feel and I love how she makes my life so much more meaningful. The things I neglected are things I don't care about.

I do need to care though unless I want to deal with constant pressure from my family.

I guess I can see Nerissa without interacting with her.

I can find out what she is doing while she's been so quiet today. It'll be like it always was - me watching from a distance, quiet and thoughtful.

The idea relaxes me. I forgot how much I used to love watching her. Yes, that's what I need to do. That will help me refocus and calm down.

Opening the app on my phone I check to see where she is located.

She's at home. According to today's timeline she's been home all day. I glance at my watch. It's four o'clock in the afternoon. It's not common for her to be home all day like this. Not since she finished her studies.

Maybe she needs me.

I rush downstairs to my car and climb in as fast as I can.

There is some traffic through the city which aggravates me to no end. My patience is thin today. I just want to get to her.

I park outside her apartment window, out of sight if she looks out onto the street. Then I open my phone and connect to her phone, turning her microphone on so I can hear what is going on in her apartment.

It's risky because if she looks at her phone, she will see that it's turned on, but it's a risk I'm ok with taking at this point. It's also something I can only do when I am in a certain radius to her.

I place the phone on my dashboard and lean back in my seat, my eyes on her window. I can see movement inside her apartment.

Hayley's voice comes through loud and clear on my speaker.

"So, the job fell through. Ok. That's horrible. But where have you been? What have you been doing? You haven't just been sitting in this apartment day after day sulking."

Her friend is being aggressive. I don't like the way she is talking to her. I clench my jaw, wanting to march up to her apartment and give her friend a piece of my mind. No one speaks to Nerissa like that.

I don't move though. I just wait. Wondering how Nerissa will handle this.

"I met a guy."

I didn't expect that.

Leaning forward in my seat my eyes are on my phone now. I am riveted. Completely invested in this conversation. I knew there was a reason my instincts were telling me to come here.

They continue talking. Nerissa is being interrogated by her friend. But I don't care anymore. I want to know as well. I have the same questions. I need this insight into Nerissa's mind.

"Are you in love, Nerissa?" Hayley says, sounding stunned by the realization.

My hands are clenched over the steering wheel. I watch the shadows move in her apartment.

There is a pause. Too long.

My heart is racing.

Nerissa's voice comes through my phone.

"It's getting — I — " She sighs, pausing. I am holding my breath, and I can't seem to let it out. I am desperate to hear her answer.

"I am falling for him."

My fists unclench and I flop backwards into my seat letting out a loud, heavy breath of relief.

She's falling for me.

Everything I have ever wanted is coming together how I planned. And this is before she even realizes she's pregnant. Once she finds out she's carrying my baby, there will be no turning back.

I spend the rest of the afternoon listening to their conversation. Much of it revolves around me, offering a revealing opportunity to delve deeper into understanding her. A significant portion pertains to her work and her anxieties about the future. But I am not interested in that. I will take care of her. I don't even want her to work because it will take time away from us being together.

Outside the sky grows darker.

I'm not going anywhere.

I'll wait all night if I have to, but I need to go in and talk to her. I want to see her face and touch her skin. She admitted how she feels about me and it's making me crazy with need for her.

Hayley only leaves her apartment well after ten o'clock. I continue to wait. Do I tell Nerissa that I know she loves me? I watch her getting ready for bed. She stands at the window, peering into the darkness. Then closes her curtains. This shocks me because she never closes her curtains. What is she up to?

Not needing to worry about being hidden anymore I move my car closer to her apartment. I am parked right under the streetlight, still listening to her phone. She isn't speaking, but the sounds of her moving around inside her apartment are soothing to me. It's as though I am in there with her, just being close to her.

I also want to wait and see if there is a reason she closed her curtains. Is she hiding something - or someone?

I hear shuffling and Nerissa climbing out of bed again. I sit tensely. What is she doing in there?

The curtains open and her beautiful face is perfectly framed in the window.

She is looking directly at me.

Her eyes are locked onto me.

She knows I am here. She knows I am watching.

My heart is beating in my chest. Will she be angry?

She steps away from the window, and I wait. I wait to hear her door opening. I want for her to rush out onto the street and come marching towards me. I wait for her to yell at me I'm crazy, a stalker, obsessed -

But instead, I hear her climbing back into bed.

I shake my head in disbelief. She knows I'm here and she's just ignoring it. Or does she like the fact that I'm watching her?

Confusion settles over me. Does she want me to go inside? Is that why the curtains are open?

I've never had her catch me before and I'm frozen with indecision.

I sit for over an hour, trying to make a choice.

Finally, I give in to my desires.

I want to see her. And I always get what I want.

Climbing out of my car I close the door. The street is pitch dark and midnight silent. There isn't a soul walking around. This isn't the best part of town and people know better than to be walking around here after dark.

I slip my hand into my pocket and pull out the copy I made of her apartment key when she moved in here. I let myself into the foyer, the security guard is fast asleep as he always is once he's locked up for the night.

I take the stairs, tiptoeing up to her front door.

Slipping the key into the lock my heart is pounding with excitement. I love the rush. I am the predator, and she is my prey. She is the most delightful creature to be hunting, and I know I will never tire of her.

I let myself into her apartment. Silent. Careful.

I walk over to the side of her bed. She is sleeping, but she looks restless.

Sitting down on the armchair that is already pulled close to the side of the bed I watch her. My future wife. The mother of my unborn child.

My everything.

She tosses and turns and mumbles my name.

I smile in the darkness, loving the fact that even in her dreams she is thinking of me.

It's difficult to stop myself from reaching out to touch her.

She rolls over again, and the blanket pulls off her, the oversized tee shirt she is wearing drifts up over her stomach so that I can see her hips, the pale pink panties she is wearing and the toned shape of her abs.

I clench my jaw.

My cock stirs.

Let her sleep, Tuomo. Soon she will be in your bed, soon you will have her every day. Just let her sleep.

She rolls over again, so restless tonight, and sighs. Her back is facing me, and my eyes are exploring the curve of her waist and the dimples above her ass.

Let her sleep, Tuomo.

CHAPTER TWENTY-FOUR
Nerissa

I climb back into bed, but my heart is racing.

He's out there. He's watching me or waiting for something.

I should be terrified but I'm not.

This isn't normal behavior though and my reaction to his behavior isn't normal either. Why would I like the fact that he is stalking me?

I sigh, rolling over and pulling the covers up over my head.

Is there something wrong with me?

Why does this turn me on?

Dammit, Nerissa. You've fallen for a tall dark and handsome giant red flag and you're too stupid to stop it from happening.

I don't know whether I should stay awake and wait for him to creep into my room. He knows how to get in here. He got in just fine on the night of my party.

I sit up suddenly filled with anxiety.

How many times has he been in here?

And if I was right about the sensation of him watching me today - how many times have I been right in the past?

Has he been following me the entire time?

He knows so much about me - it seems obvious. But I guess I wanted to turn a blind eye to this alarming truth about him.

Despite that, even now - I *like* it.

I like the fact that he is so fascinated by me. I enjoy being wanted by someone to the point of them needing to be around me so much.

Am I really that special to him? The man who could have any girl his heart desires.

I lie back down, staring up at the ceiling, trying to count all the times I thought I felt him near me.

This is evidence of how dangerous he is. And in all honesty, it should have me calling the cops.

So, why am I just lying here waiting for him?

Did he leave when he saw me looking out the window?

What does this mean?

I have so many questions pulsing through my mind. I'm jittery and unable to find peace, my mind racing. I can't lie here forever waiting for someone who might not even be there anymore. I should get up and check.

No.

I can't.

I could message him.

No.

Leave it alone. Don't encourage it.

You know it's wrong.

I grab my pillow and press it over my face, forcing myself to close my eyes.

I need to sleep. Tomorrow, I need to find a job. Tuomo is not healthy for me and tonight proves that even more. He's who I thought he was - dangerous - risky.

So, then why am I fantasizing about him breaking in here and doing whatever he wants to me?

"Dammit, Nerissa." I whisper into my pillow.

I'm losing myself. Or I've already lost myself. Either way I am in *way* too deep - and everything happened so fast. It's like he orchestrated the entire thing, manipulating me every step of the way.

I'm not even sure what he is really capable of.

It's like I want to test his limits. I want to test how far he would go. But I don't really want to find out though. The fantasy of having a guy stalking you is so much sexier than having him stalk you.

What would my mother think of all of this? She'd be so angry with me for letting it get this far. And even Hayley. If I had told her the truth about who he is - and how I thought, he was following me - she would have had me committed to a psych ward.

Tossing and turning I'm overwhelmed, and guilty, and scared, and turned on -

I don't know how or when, but I fall asleep and of course, I dream of him.

His hands are on my body as I roll over in bed. He is lying next to me. He smiles when I look up at him. I should scream, but I don't. My silence is like an invitation.

His hand travels up over my side, heating my skin wherever it touches. I moan and he pulls me closer. His cock is hard against my naked body, and I'm tingling with desire.

My breath catches when he presses his lips against mine. His hand locks around my throat as he rolls onto me.

"Wait—" I whisper. This is wrong. I shouldn't let this happen. I shouldn't want this. But I spread my legs, another invite.

His dark eyes are on me, penetrating my soul. I feel as though he is possessing me, my body no longer belongs to me, and he can do whatever he wishes to it.

He pushes my face to the side, pressing it hard against the pillow and leans forward to whisper against my ear. His deep voice is a threatening growl that makes my pussy throb with desire.

"You belong to me, little bird."

I gasp, fighting against the unknown of what he plans to do with me.

His hand is between my thighs, his fingers pushing into me.

My eyes flutter closed as pleasure floods me.

Then I feel his cock. His monstrous cock, rubbing over my pussy.

I rock my hips upwards against him, trying to guide him into me.

He chuckles. A deliciously dark sound that vibrates through my entire body sending shivers down my spine.

"Tuomo." I call out his name like a drug on my lips.

He moves against me, pushing inside me. It is indescribable. I moan louder, digging my nails into his skin, wanting everything.

He pushes deep into me, and I can barely breathe.

My eyes shoot open, and I lie dead still in my bed. I'm facing the wall, trying to keep my breathing even. Trying to stay as quiet as possible to not give away the fact that I am no longer sleeping.

Is he here?

Is he in my room?

What woke me up?

My heart is racing. It could be from my dream. I can feel the layer of perspiration on my chest, heated desire spilling over into the real world.

I want to roll over and look around my room, but I'm frozen in place.

What do I do if he really is in my room?

The darkness is heavy and ominous. I shouldn't be this scared of him, but I am. I don't know what he's capable of.

Should I say his name? Will he answer me?

The tension of not knowing if I'm alone is making my entire body rigid with fear.

Every cell in my body is alert. Adrenaline is coursing through my blood like molten lava. I can't just lie here forever. I need to do something.

If he was going to do something bad, he would have done it already.

I take a deep breath, willing myself to roll over and scan the rest of the room. The darkness makes it hard to see and even the shape of my jacket in the corner, hanging from the closet handle, looks like it could be something else.

I'm being ridiculous. It was just the dream that made me wake up.

I shift my body, waiting, nothing happens.

Gathering all my courage I roll over onto my back and immediately I see him.

A scream building in the back of my throat and bursts through my lips, loud and piercing through the still darkness of my room.

In a flash he moves over me, reaching out he clamps his hand over my face.

I struggle, kicking out and tangling myself in the blankets. Panic removes all reason, and I fight hard against him as he presses me into the bed.

I don't stop. I don't give up.

He climbs onto the bed, kneeling over me so that I am trapped beneath him.

I scream against his hand, but the sound is muffled and pointless.

"Stop." He shouts, pressing down harder until my face hurts.

"Nerissa, stop." He snarls angrily.

I can't breathe and I can't move. I freeze, staring up at him with wide eyes, pleading him to let me go.

CHAPTER TWENTY-FIVE
Tuomo

She is fighting and kicking underneath me. I squeeze my knees together trying to give her less movement. Desperate to calm her down. The blankets are knotted over her, and she is only making it worse for herself. She screams again against my hand, and I am forced to push harder over her mouth. This is turning me on. I could rip her panties off and thrust into her right now. She doesn't stand a chance against me. I close my eyes for a second, not letting her go.

"Stop." I growl, not wanting to lose control of myself and hurt her. She knew I was outside, she knew I was here. Why the fuck is she acting so terrified? She kicks again and scratches her nails across my arm.

"Nerissa, stop." I say with threat in my voice.

Finally, she freezes, she stops kicking. In fact, she stops moving all together.

In the heavy silence that falls over the room I can feel her pulse beating fast against my hand. Her body is shaking beneath me.

"It's *me*, for crying out loud." I sigh heavily. "I'm going to take my hand off your mouth now. Are you going to keep quiet?" she nods, her eyes locked onto me.

I lift my hand. Even in the dark I can see the red outline of where my fingers were locked onto her face.

She doesn't move, and she doesn't make a sound.

I sit up, still kneeling over her, but not needing to use the weight of my body to keep her quiet anymore. Her breathing is still heavy and sharp. Each breath she takes is loud, breaking the silence.

"Are you ok?" I ask after giving her a moment.

She nods.

I climb off her, even though I don't want to. I take a seat in the armchair again, rubbing my hands over my face.

"I thought you knew I was here." I sigh.

She sits up, scrambling back against the headboard and pulling the blankets up over herself to hide her legs. I wish she hadn't. I could pull the blanket away, but I won't. I need to give her a moment.

"I - I saw you outside." She mutters.

"I'm going to make you some tea." I say, standing up, moving so I don't startle her again.

She leans over and flicks on the row of fairy lights that are hanging across the corner of her room. Soft warm light fills the space, and it soothes away some of the tension.

"I'm sorry." I say, running my hand through my hair. "I didn't mean to give you a fright."

"It's ok." She says, not looking at me. She is busy trying to straighten the knotted blanket.

I pull two mugs out of her kitchen cupboard and filled the kettle, turning it on.

Then I watch her while I wait for it to boil.

She's up now, remaking her bed, hurrying as though she has tension she needs to shake off. She bends over to pull the blankets straight and the t-shirt slips up over her ass. I snarl. She is teasing me. She is doing that on purpose.

But I can see that's not true. She's too stressed to be thinking about that right now.

She sits back down on the bed and crosses her legs, placing a pillow on her lap as though it will comfort her. A shield between me and her body.

The pillow wouldn't help anything if I decided not to behave. But if it makes her feel better it really doesn't matter.

The kettle clicks and I put hot water over the tea bags, watching them bleed ochre, red into the water like a strange dance.

I splash a little milk into each mug and a spoon of sugar, then carry them both back to the armchair, sitting down. She takes the mug from me and sips it, testing the heat.

"Are you sure you're ok?" I ask, wondering if I hurt her.

"I'm alright." She says, touching her fingertips against her lips.

I grab her jaw and turn her face towards me. The red mark is still there. A tinge of guilt and a surge of lust hits me at the same time. I love to see my mark on her. But I don't want to cause her pain she doesn't enjoy.

I lean back in the chair.

"Why were you watching me?" She asks, her eyes piercing into me.

"Because I needed to make sure you were ok. I haven't heard from you today."

"You could have messaged me."

"Why didn't you do anything when you saw me outside your window?" I turn the question back onto her.

She bites her lips and sighs. "I - I don't know."

"Hayley was here earlier. What did you guys talk about?"

"Life. Work. Things I'm worried about." She shrugs.

"What are you worried about, Nerissa?"

She takes another sip of tea and then puts the mug down on her bedside table.

"Everything." She huffs, throwing her hands in the air.

I shake my head. "Didn't I tell you that as long as you are with me there is nothing, I won't do for you?"

"And I told you I don't believe in fairytales." She pulls her mouth to the side.

A chuckle falls from my lips. "Sweet girl, this isn't a fairytale. I am very real, and I am sitting right here - and I will do anything for you."

She squints at me, and I can see her thoughts fluttering across her eyes. She wants to believe me, but something is holding her back.

"Talk to me." I say, reaching out and touching her leg.

"I don't know why everyone is turning down my applications to work at their law firms. I don't know what to do with my life if the thing I studied becomes useless because no one will hire me."

"I can talk to some people I work with and get you a job if that will make you happy."

"I don't want someone to give me a job just because of your influence. I want to earn it for myself." She sighs. "What happens when you get bored with me and walk away - what happens to me then? I get sacked."

"Get bored with you? Are you crazy? It's been seven years since I met you and not a single day has gone by when I haven't wanted you. Why would that change, little bird?"

I put my tea down and sit on the bed next to her. Wrapping my arms around her waist I pull her against me. The pillow falls from her lap, and she leans into me, letting me hold her. Her heart is calmer now. I can still feel the steady rhythm of it against my body, but she is no longer afraid of me. I stroke my hand down her back, letting my fingers thread through her hair.

"Nerissa, whatever challenges life throws at us - I want to face them together. I want us to be together."

"But you come from such a different world to me. Our lives are not the same. You never have to worry about money or whether you'll be ok in the future."

"And when you are with me, you won't have to worry about that either."

She wiggles in my arms so that she can lift her head and look up at me. Her hazel eyes look dark green in the soft light. As beautiful as ever. I place my finger beneath her chin, then lean down to kiss her. Her lips are warm against mine and as soon as my mouth locks over hers I want her all over again.

I pull her onto my lap, wrapping her legs around my hips.

She moans, moving over me, rocking against me.

Running my hands up her thighs I savor the sweet taste of tea in her mouth.

Cupping her ass cheeks in my hands I pull her harder against my cock.

Suddenly her apartment door opens and three dark figures rush in. I throw her off me, onto the bed, standing up to create a blockage between whoever they are and her. I will die fighting to protect her. No one touches her but me.

Nerissa isn't screaming this time, but I can hear her sharp squeal of surprise and the way her breath catches in her throat.

"Stay behind me." I snarl.

She scampers off the bed and ducks behind it.

The figures step closer and to my absolute shock I see my brothers staring at me.

"What the fuck?" I stammer, standing up straight, relaxing, but not having even the slightest clue what the hell is going on.

"Tuomo." Masaccio says, glaring at me. Rufino's fists are clenched at his side. He doesn't seem to know if he's here to fight or not. "Who is that girl?" Masaccio asks, lifting his chin and gesturing towards Nerissa.

"She is none of your concern." I reply with force. I don't need them knowing who she is. If they find out, there will be all hell to pay because I will have to explain it all to my father.

"She very much is our concern because I'm damned sure she is the reason you've been acting so weird."

"Just leave it alone, brother." I warn him, taking a step towards him. All three of them step close to me and I'm in trouble.

CHAPTER TWENTY-SIX
Nerissa

The door flies open, and my adrenaline shoots up again. Tuomo throws me behind himself and stands to defend me. I'm terrified, but he will protect me.

I don't even scream. There is no point. My neighbors don't care.

"Stay behind me." Tuomo commands.

I scamper off the bed, over the edge and onto the floor, ducking low and peaking up to see what is going on.

The three dark shadows who burst into my room step closer and light touches their faces.

I gasp.

I know who they are.

I would recognize the Vece brothers anywhere.

They all look older, more defined, stronger - but it is them.

But what the hell are they doing in my apartment in the middle of the night.

Tuomo is just as shocked as I am, and they argue. I don't know if I should stand up and tell them all to calm down or just stay out of it.

Masaccio seems the most upset, and Rufino seems ready to tear Tuomo apart. Celso is hanging near the back, not saying much, trying to stay out of the fight.

"You need to leave." Tuomo hisses. "You have no right to be here."

"We aren't going anywhere until we know who that girl is and what you are doing with her. Is she a hooker? Does she have something on you? If she's blackmailing—"

"Fuck off man. She isn't a hooker. Nothing is going on here that you need to be involved in."

Rufino marches over to the wall and flicks on the main light.

Harsh bright light floods the room, and I lift my hand over my eyes blinking at the sudden intrusion. Shit. I'm not even wearing pants and there are four men in my room.

"Stand up." Masaccio demands.

I hesitate. I don't know what to do.

Masaccio makes as though he is going to walk around the bed towards me and Tuomo steps in front of him, pushing his hands against his brother's chest to stop him.

"Leave her the fuck alone."

"Get out of my way before I take you down, Tuomo. We are sick and tired of your shit, and we need to know what the fuck is going on."

Rufino steps forward and grabs Tuomo's arm. He is much bigger than Tuomo. And while Tuomo could take many men down, Rufino looks as though he could crush a truck with his fist.

Masaccio steps past Tuomo as he struggles in Rufino's grasp.

He walks to the bed and glares down at me.

"No." he mutters. "It can't be." His mouth drops open as he stares down at me.

"Who is it?" Rufino and Celso ask.

I stare at Tuomo, begging him for help with my eyes.

He closes his eyes and his jaw clenches. He knows there is no way out of this.

I stand up, pulling the edges of my t-shirt down, as low as it will go, so I'm completely exposed.

"Nerissa?" Rufino gasps in shock. "The maid's kid?"

Celso pushes past his two brothers to stare at me and I feel like I'm on display for all of them. I'm vulnerable and very alone in this moment.

"Guys, please, leave her alone." Tuomo says.

Masaccio turns on him with anger. "Are you fucking stupid? How many times did our father have to warn you to stay away from her. She is beneath you. She is trouble. What the fuck are you doing messing with her?"

Tuomo's rage surges and he shoves Rufino off him. Rufino lets go and steps away. It's not like Tuomo can fight all of them - but right now it looks as though he will try.

"I said get out." He snarls.

Masaccio steps towards him and grabs his shirt in both hands, growling into his face.

"What the fuck are you doing here, Tuomo? Who is she to you?"

Tuomo's breathing is heavy. I can see his chest heaving up and down.

"She is the woman I love." He whispers, but his voice is steady and strong.

"Love?" Masaccio stammers in shock. "You think you love her?"

"I don't fucking *think* I love her - I know I do."

"Dad's going to kill him." Rufino says, shaking his head.

I am just standing there like a mute statue, not sure what to do. I want to defend Tuomo. But I feel attacked myself. Who cares if my mother was a cleaner. She was an incredible woman. A kind, loving, and gentle person who deserves respect. My fists clench at my side. They are all horrible people. They are nasty and cruel, and I want them out of my house.

But I don't say a damned thing.

I'm too scared.

"Leave our father out of this." Tuomo says, his eyes darkening towards Masaccio and Rufino. Celso sighs. "We don't have to tell dad. It will turn into a nightmare if we do."

"Shut up, Celso. Nobody asked you. This is a serious situation. If you will not help us - leave."

"Fuck sakes, don't be an asshole, I was just saying that we can handle this between ourselves." Celso turns towards Tuomo. "Bro, you can't get away with dating someone like her. Stop. If you agree to stay away from her, we don't have to tell dad anything. He has an entire plan, a list of possible, suitable wives for us."

"I will never let her go. Since the day I met her, I decided she would be my wife, and I don't care if I have to fight every single one of you to make that clear." Tuomo is furious and not backing down.

Masaccio is getting tense and Rufino's brows are so knotted it looks as though he wants to tear Tuomo apart.

Rufino turns to Masaccio. "We should deal with this in private." He gestures towards me, eyeing me as though I was a spy.

"You're right. Tuomo, come with us."

"Fuck you." He snarls.

"Rufino." Masaccio nods.

Rufino steps forward with purpose and grabs Tuomo's arms. "It's time to go, man."

Tuomo fights and Masaccio steps into the mess of arms and legs and between the two of them they clamp him in a head lock.

Still - I don't move. I'm frozen. I'm terrified.

Rufino drags Tuomo out of my apartment and away from me.

Masaccio stands alone after everyone else has left. His eyes are dark on me. Threatening.

He steps close to me. Close enough that I can smell his breath against my face when he speaks.

"If you speak a word about our family to anyone, I will make sure you never see the light of day again. I don't know what was going on between you two - but it's over now."

My heart is beating so fast I can hear it in my ears. I'm holding my breath. Too afraid to move.

"Nod if you understand, girl."

I nod and take a shuddering breath in.

He grabs my jaw in his hand and pulls my face closer to his.

"I never want to see you again." He snarls.

Then he lets me go and walks out.

My apartment is empty and silent again.

I stare at the open door, willing myself to rush forward and close it.

I take a long time to find the ability to move again.

When I do I close the door, with shaking hands and tears in my eyes.

I am so grateful that none of them saw me crying - that I held back all of my emotions until they were gone.

I walk backwards until my legs bump against my bed then I sit down.

For over an hour I just sit there staring at the door. I don't know if I'm safe. I don't know if one of them is going to come back for me and make sure that I can't tell them anything. I don't even know anything. Tuomo didn't speak about his family. What is there to tell?

Focus on your breathing, deep slow breaths in and out. They aren't coming back.

But still. I stare at the door.

I stare at the door until light filters in through my window and only then do I lie down on the bed and close my eyes - too exhausted to think anymore. Too exhausted to worry if someone is going to come crashing through the door to steal me away and make me disappear.

My dreams are dark and full of dangerous things.

I was asking for trouble getting involved with Tuomo.

I should never have done it and now - now my heart is aching, and I'm scared for my life.

CHAPTER TWENTY-SEVEN
Tuomo

Halfway down the stairs leaving her apartment I stop fighting against Rufino. At this point there is no chance of me getting away from them and back to her. They won't let it happen.

With deep reluctance I walk. I made the choices I made and now I have to face the consequences of those choices.

But no matter what happens I will not give her up.

In no life, on no planet, and in no timeline, I am not meant to be with Nerissa.

"Fuck." Rufino complains, walking just behind me as we leave the building. "I'm going to have a bruise." I glance back at him and he's rubbing his jaw.

Good.

He shouldn't have interfered. I am going to be bruised in few spots as well. My shoulders are so tight they ache, and I might have pulled my back trying to wrestle away from Rufino's grip. I rub my hand over my ribs, testing to see which is the most tender.

Rufino pulls the door open. "Get in."

"I'll take my car."

"Like fuck. Get in."

I shake my head but slide onto the back seat. He holds out his hand and I toss my car keys to him.

"Celso, bring his car back." He says, throwing the keys to Celso.

Masaccio hasn't come out of the building yet and my protective instinct is kicking into gear.

"If he hurts her—"

"He will not hurt her. He's just going to make sure she understands to stay away." Rufino sighs, sliding into the back seat next to me.

I can't take it anymore. How long has Masaccio been in there alone with her and what is he doing? I put my hand on the door handle and just as I'm about to get out of the car - Masaccio walks out of the building. He looks calm.

I glare at him, looking for any signs of a struggle. Blood. Torn clothes.

He climbs into the car and looks back at me.

"What did you do?" I snap.

"She's fine. We just had a polite conversation." The engine of his car growls to life, and he speeds up so fast the tires scream against the road.

Celso pulls out behind us and follows us to my father's mansion.

I don't say a word. There's nothing to say.

We arrive at the mansion and my father is waiting on the top step in front of the open door.

He looks furious.

"Fuck." I mutter under my breath.

"Don't do anything stupid." Rufino says sounding concerned.

I climb out of the car and follow my brothers past my father's heated glare into the house.

He walks in behind us and slams the door closed.

"The dead fucking maid's daughter?" he snarls in anger. "The same girl that I got rid of years ago?"

I turn to face him. Apparently, we are doing this right here in the entrance hall.

"Yes." I say, plain and simple.

"I made myself very clear when I told you to stay away from that trash."

I shake my head. How dare he speak about her like that?

Times have changed. I am not the same man I was all those years ago. I was still scared of him back then. I had respect for his power. All I have now is hatred.

"Don't ever speak about her like that. And don't for a second think that you have a right to tell me who I can fall in love with."

"Love?" he packs up laughing. His cruelty shining through in every way.

"Yes. I love her. I have always loved her."

"You can't love someone you haven't seen in six years you, idiot."

I shake my head, a smile across my face. "I've seen her every day of my life for the past six years. You never kept me away from her."

My father snarls and steps towards me with clenched fists.

"You disobeyed me?"

"I did."

He glares at me with eyes full of rage. He spits his words into my face. "You want to be with trash because you are trash. It doesn't even matter. *You* don't matter. You have always been a disappointment. Nothing has changed."

Even though I hate my father, his words of rejection cut deep into me.

Pain and a deep need to defend myself again years of his abuse overwhelm me to where I am no longer in control.

He's pushed me too far. This is the final straw.

I fly at him, taking everyone in the room by surprise, including myself.

My fist slams into his jaw, I hear his teeth crashing together at the impact of my punch.

He staggers backwards, a look of total awe on his face - maybe even respect.

But then his eyes turn dark, and he comes flying back at me.

I tackle him to the ground, ducking low and using his own momentum against him when he reaches me, I punch my shoulder into his stomach and throw him backwards. He hits the ground with a heavy thud, and I don't even hesitate to carry on attacking.

Blow after blow my fists connect with his face.

Years of hurt.

Years of anger.

It all comes pouring out of me in a blind rage.

I don't even think I can stop. I might kill him.

Powerful hands grab me and rip me backwards. "Stop." Rufino shouts. Masaccio runs towards my father who shoves him away, embarrassed and bleeding.

"Get him away from me before I shoot him." My father spits blood onto the marble floor.

Masaccio turns to Rufino. "Take him to the warehouse."

"The fucking warehouse. Are you fucking kidding me?" I scream, kicking against his grip. But it's no use. I spent my energy on my father. I fought with everything I had, and I took him down.

As a kid I never thought there would come a day when I would be stronger than him, but I've just proven to myself that I am.

I will never fear him again.

Not physically.

But he has other sources of power. And if I'm not careful, I don't think he would hesitate to make me disappear. He doesn't even see me as a son, so what difference would it make to him? As long as he has his precious first born the world is all good for him.

Rufino throws me into the back of the car again and sits next to me. He is fuming.

I turn my eyes out of the opposite window. I don't care.

I don't care about any of them.

They can all burn in hell.

I want Nerissa and they won't be able to stop me.

I don't care if they disown me and deny ever knowing me.

All I want is her. She is all that matters.

Masaccio climbs into the car and we drive to the warehouse in silence.

It's heavy and tense.

When he parks the car, before he gets out, he speaks to me without turning around.

"You should never have done that."

"I did what I had to. Someone had to show that old fool that he doesn't have all the power."

"But he does, Tuomo. He has all the power and now you've triggered him. You do not know what he is going to do in revenge."

I clench my jaw.

"Don't let him hurt her?" I say, desperate and foolish.

"I can't promise anything."

They drag me to the basement of the warehouse and throw me into a holding cell.

"You can't be serious. You aren't really going to leave me here?" I stammer in disbelief.

"We are. But I'll come and check on you tomorrow. I'm sorry but you have given us no choice. You need to sort your head out, you've lost it. Some alone time to think will be good for you." Masaccio turns and walks away, followed by Rufino. They leave one light on and no matter how many times I scream for them to stop - neither of them turns around and comes back.

I slump against the cold concrete floor. This can't be happening.

The reality of what I've done crashes into me.

My father is so furious, and he might do something to Nerissa. He will hurt her.

I have to get out of here and warn her. I can give her money, and she can disappear. I put her in so much danger because I was too stupid to control myself.

I'm a fucking idiot.

The cold, empty space suffocates me as I sit alone, waiting for morning, waiting for someone to come and tell me they changed their mind - that I can go home.

But I'm waiting for nothing and no one.

And when morning comes my brothers still don't show up.

CHAPTER TWENTY-EIGHT
Nerissa

Another day goes by, and I don't hear from Tuomo. His brothers dragged him out of my apartment two days ago and I don't know what to make of it. I imagine his brothers were so angry to find him with someone like me he was told he can't see me again. He knew all along that it wouldn't work but just wanted to play out whatever fantasy he had in his head about me.

There have been so many times when I've wanted to message him, but I've stopped myself.

What happened that night was terrifying, and I don't want my life to be like that.

His family hates me.

I have no idea what they would do to me if they found out I was trying to get in touch with him again. And apart from that obvious fact - I don't have any idea what to say to him. It's not like I can just message *hi, how are you, what you been up to.*

But I miss him. I ache to have his arms around me and hear his voice. I want to lie down with my head on his chest and feel the soothing beat of his heart.

Though - nothing is more important than family and even though Tuomo said he would take them all down to be with me - I would never ask or expect him to lose his family over me. Nobody should be forced into a position to make that choice, so I have to be strong enough to make it for him if it stops him from losing his family. I couldn't live with myself anyway - if that happened.

I slide my phone back into the back pocket of my jeans for the hundredth time. And for the hundredth time I reassure myself I've made the right choice not to message him. It's so hard though. My heart is breaking. But I also have to acknowledge that he hasn't messaged me either. Looking up and down the busy street I sigh.

He must know that it is impossible for us to be together. He must have known all along.

It's time we both accepted the truth and just walked away before things get so much worse than they already are.

I'm already embarrassed to pass any of my neighbors in the hallway because of the mayhem I have been causing there. It's not who I am. I am the level-headed quiet girl who focuses on studies and work.

I'm not built to be involved with a mafia boss.

I step into the street and hurry across the road when there is a gap in the traffic.

I called Hayley an hour ago because I've been sitting at home doing nothing but crying. It's making me crazy. I've just arrived at the coffee shop she is meeting me at. I'm early, but I couldn't wait in my apartment for another second. So, I'd rather sit here than there. At least here I can watch people, and I don't feel so alone.

Being alone right now scares me. Especially in that apartment. The Vece brothers know where I live, and the threat was very clear. I am still worried about them coming back to find me and just - *get rid of me.* It seems over the top and unrealistic, like something from a horror movie, but that's the family they are. I've heard all the rumors, I lived in their home, and I met their father. He is a horrible, horrible man.

I order a cappuccino from the pretty waitress who leads me to a table by the window. She looks about seventeen - the same age I was when I first fell for Tuomo. She looks like a child, far too young to be making any big decision that will affect the rest of her life.

I wonder if people thirty-five or forty see me and think I'm a child - like I am too young to make important choices. And then do fifty-year-olds look at the thirty-year-olds and think the same thing. Are we ever really able to make big choices with the way life throws curveballs at us? How can we prepare for things we can't even guess are going to happen to us?

If I look at all the choices, I've made so far, they have all gotten me nowhere in my life.

I don't have a job even though I did so well in university.

I'm a wreck. A heartbroken mess. Living alone in an apartment I won't be able to pay rent for when my savings run out in two months.

A tear rolls down my cheek and the lump in my throat forces me to swallow hard.

"Here's your cappa - oh my goodness are you ok?" the waitress squats down next to my table and reaches up to touch my shoulder. "Honey, are you ok?" She asks.

I smile through my tears, nodding. "I'm fine. Just, um, just silly problems with silly boys." I shrug, embarrassed that she is comforting me. I don't want to draw any attention to myself.

"Oh babe, I know that hurt. They can be a real pain - but one day you'll meet one who will sweep you off your feet."

I laugh. "You're a little young to let guys sweep you off your feet, aren't you?"

She giggles and holds out her hand, showing me a gorgeous ring. "No, I've already met my prince charming. We've been in love since junior school. He asked me to marry him a month ago."

Tears spill again. She is so much younger than me and somehow, she has her life together, a job, a man who wants to marry her and she looks thrilled.

"That's amazing." I say, wishing she would leave me alone to wallow in my self-pity.

I didn't even ask to fall in love.

It wasn't a choice I made. It just came out of nowhere - hijacking my life and creating chaos for me. But here I am - in love with a Vece - with no idea how to handle it.

"What's going on?" Hayley's voice makes the waitress jump.

"Boy trouble." She says, standing and smiling at Hayley. "Can I bring you a coffee too?"

"Yes, thanks." Hayley says, pulling out a chair and scooting it right next to mine.

She wraps her arms around my shoulders and hugs me.

"What did he do? I'll kill him."

I shake my head, taking a deep breath and trying to get myself under control. "No, it's better that we break up. We shouldn't have been together."

"But I thought you really liked him."

"I did - but I knew he wasn't right for me. I don't even want to talk about it now. Can we leave that conversation for another day? I just want to forget about it and have a pleasant afternoon with you."

Hayley narrows her eyes at me for a moment then sighs. "Ok, yes, let's cheer you up - but you are going to tell me what happened at some point right?"

"I will. I promise. Just not today."

She nods. "Alright. We can have coffee - and then we can go to the little market in the park today. It's a bunch of vintage and thrift stuff. It'll be fun to shop around."

"That sounds perfect."

The young waitress returns with Hayley's cappuccino and smiles at me. I glance down at her hand, at the pretty ring on her fingers. Is that what I want? Do I want to get married? What a crazy thought. All I have ever focused on was work and trying to make a good life for myself. Now suddenly I am crying over a guy and questioning everything because it all fell apart.

The waitress walks away, and I look back at Hayley.

"Now isn't a good time to tell you - but you want a distraction, right?" she grins.

"I want a distraction. And you can tell me anything."

"I got a job. A proper one. I'm working as a clerk in the office at that law firm in town - with the big blue statue outside their building."

"I know which one that is. That's amazing. Oh, my word I am so proud of you."

"I wanted to tell you yesterday when they emailed me, but I decided to rather tell you in person."

We chat about her future and all the potential that working in a place like that will bring. I applied there. I remember they told me they weren't looking to hire anyone right now. But I don't tell Hayley that. She is my best friend, and I want the world for her. I want everything good for her.

After our coffee we walk the long way to the park, enjoying the city energy and taking our time, just filling the day with nothing.

The vintage market is beautiful. There are so many fun treasures to look at, for a little while I forget about everything that happened and how broken my heart is.

But that loneliness creeps in as the afternoon grows late.

I think again about how I want to message him but knowing I can't.

I'm empty, even spending time with such an amazing friend, because the only person I really want to be with right now is Tuomo.

CHAPTER TWENTY-NINE
Tuomo

For two days I was locked in that basement underneath the warehouse and for two days my brothers visited me, taking it in turns to convince me I should change my mind about her. They were begging me to 'see reason.' But what reason is there to convince me of.

I love her. She is incredible.

I don't care what her mother did for a living or where she was born and what her blood line is. I love her and that is all that matters.

My stubborn commitment to her infuriates them but I won't let go. If this is some kind of test of my love for her, I won't fail it.

It is just past lunch time on the second day when Celso comes in carrying take outs and two beers.

He unlocks the holding cell and walks inside, sitting down on the floor near me.

"Dude, I don't even want to talk about your girl." He sighs, reaching into the bag and pulling out a burger and fries for himself - then handing me the bag.

It smells great. He hands me a beer. Ice cold.

I eye him suspiciously.

"What is this? Good cop bad cop?" I ask, wondering what games he is playing. "Some kind of manipulation?"

He shakes his head, his mouth full of burger.

After chewing his food, he shakes his head again. "No, man. I just don't get what the fuss is about. Who the fuck cares who you fall in love with?" He shrugs, taking a swig from his beer. "They act like who we marry is so important. It's not."

I twist the cap off mine and take two long gulps. It's ice cold and refreshing as it rushes down my throat.

Celso doesn't speak much while we eat our burgers and drink our beers and after a while I believe him. This isn't a tactic. He doesn't give a shit about Nerissa and I being together. I know that the bigger picture is all about power — I should marry for power, to make the family stronger. My father probably has a wife picked out, the way he chose Leora for Mas.

"And dad? How has he been?"

"Ah fuck man, you pissed him off. He wants to kill you. If I was you, I would stay away from him for a while and give him a chance to calm down. You're safer in here than anywhere he can see you."

I snort a bitter laugh. "Like I have a choice. I'm locked in a fucking basement like an animal. Besides one of you three will piss him off soon enough, and he will forget I hit him."

Celso nods his head from side to side, crumpling the empty burger packet and standing up.

"Maybe. Maybe I will be the idiot who pisses him off next." He walks out of the cell, not looking back, but he says. "Maybe I was the idiot who forgot to lock the door."

He walks up the basement stairs and disappears from sight.

I can't believe it. Did he really just do that for me?

I leap to my feet and run for the door. I don't know if this is a trick - for all I know Rufino might be waiting up there to slam his fist into my throat and take me down again - but I don't care. I have to try. I need to see her.

I rush through the door and find no army waiting for me on the other side.

The warehouse is empty.

At the exit I see Celso has left my phone on the floor right in the middle of the doorway. He's a fucking legend. I never knew he had it in him to stand up against our father, but he's proven himself to be a loyal brother to me today.

I feel bad for all the times I ripped him off about having a different mom. We are half-brothers and he has treated me better than either of my actual brothers did.

I bend down and scoop my phone up off the ground.

It's even charged.

I book an Uber and then run out onto the road to wait for it. I need to get home and get changed.

Then I am going to find her.

It's almost five o'clock when I step out of my penthouse, showered, looking fresh and sharp, and ready to head over to a coffee somewhere in the city where her location is tracking.

I arrive and spot her sitting at a table near the window. I don't get out of my car though. I am very curious about who she's with and what she's doing because over the two days that I've been locked up, she hasn't messaged me.

Not once.

Not even to check that I'm ok.

I watch her interacting with Hayley.

Nerissa looks a little lost, her eyes are puffy as though she hasn't been sleeping, or she's been crying. She is smiling though and having a pleasant conversation with her friend so it's confusing for me. I can't tell if she is upset that I'm missing or not.

After a while they pay the bill and stand up, walking out together.

I climb out of my car and follow on foot.

They are laughing and joking about life and work and many things as they stroll through the city. I become more and more agitated with her.

It is disturbing to me she can be in such a good mood.

I could be dead for all she knows.

In fact, I could be locked up like an animal in a cell - and she doesn't give a shit about me.

I have to hold myself back from walking over to her and grabbing her arm and shaking her. I want to scream at her for her lack of concern. I want to know why she doesn't have a heart.

Was it all fake? Everything she said she felt about me - was it all a game to her?

She is so selfish to go on with her life like this after everything that happened.

I follow them to a market in a park. They buy cinnamon pancakes and browse the endless stalls of old things. She smiles, and chats - but when she turns in my direction, I can see how empty her eyes are.

Maybe the happiness is all an act to convince Hayley that everything is ok.

My impatience to find out is getting out of hand.

Hayley hugs Nerissa goodbye and they walk in opposite directions.

I count, staying calm and still until Hayley is too far away for me to see her.

Then I approach Nerissa, grabbing her and dragging her into a side street.

At first, she screams in fright and tries to spin away from me, but when I say her name, she gasps and turns to face me with wide, sad eyes.

"Tuomo?" She whispers. "Where have you been?"

"Where have you been, Nerissa? Having fun? Out partying? A nice day out with your friends?" I snarl.

I am so happy to see her, so happy to touch her, but I am infuriated because she doesn't give a shit about me at all.

"It's not like that and you know it." She snaps back at me, yanking her arm away from my grip.

"Then why don't you tell me what it is like, little bird."

I glare down at her and she glares right back at me.

"You want to know what it's like? It's terrifying - having three men break into your apartment in the middle of the night and steal away the person you care about. It's terrifying having one of those men threaten your life if you don't stay away from his brother and it's terrifying to have to walk around watching your back the entire time. Don't you dare come here after ignoring me for two days and pretend like I am in the wrong?"

She's furious.

I close my eyes for a second and take a deep breath.

"I'm sorry, Nerissa. You're right. That wasn't fair of me. I would have contacted you. In fact, I would have come to see you, but my brother's locked me up and wouldn't let me out. I escaped a few hours ago and then first thing I did was come find you."

"They *locked you up*?" she stammers in shock. "But you're their brother?"

I shrug. "They don't want us together."

She takes a step away from me and I grab her around the waist and pull her back towards me. "I don't care what they think, little bird. I want you. I want nothing but you. I am in love with you, Nerissa. Can't you see that?"

She shakes her head, pushing her hands against my chest. Tears stream down her cheeks.

"Please, don't say that." She begs, trying to get away from me.

"Say what?"

"That you love me. Its better if you don't say that. I can't take much more of this."

She is crying hard now, her cheeks are glowing red, and her face is scrunched up.

"But it's true. I love you. Nothing else matters. Why aren't you happy to hear that? Why don't you tell me you love me too?"

"Stop it." She shouts, distressed and still trying to push me away.

I let go of her and she takes a big step backwards. She wipes the back of her hands across her cheeks and smears the tears away.

"We can't be together, Tuomo. Isn't it obvious?"

No. No. This can't be happening. After everything we've been through. This cannot be happening.

"We are together. And nothing in the world is strong enough to break us apart." I snarl, stepping close to her again.

She sighs, shaking her head. "We aren't together. And if we were - then I have to break up with you."

Her words cut into me like a blade slicing straight into my heart. Slipping between my ribs and tearing through my flesh.

CHAPTER THIRTY
Nerissa

His eyes are darker than I have ever seen him, and he is towering over me with a menacing anger spread across his face. The heat of his skin brushes against mine and electricity bolts through me. My body burns with need, contradicting the nervous tension in my heart.

"You're breaking up with me?" he says in absolute disbelief.

"Tuomo—" I stammer, fearful of him. His anger is a dangerous thing. I've seen glimpses of it before but this time it looks worse. "Tuomo, accept that it's impossible for us to be together. You will *lose* your family. Don't you get that?"

I try to step away from him, to create some distance between us but he isn't letting me.

In the narrow alley under a sky that is growing darker by the minute he has my back pressed right up against the brick wall. I can feel the coldness of it seeping through my shirt.

"If you loved me nothing would break us apart." He whispers with menace tainting the edge of each word.

"Your *family*," I cry out. "They are your entire world."

"*You are my universe.*" He screams into my face, and I wince away from his anger.

"I can't be your world." I shout back at him, fear driving me to be more forceful.

He laughs as he runs his hand up my chest, towards my neck, wrapping his fingers around my throat. He pushes me back hard against the wall again and pain shoots through my back.

"I will never give up. I will never ever let you get away from me, Nerissa. I don't want anyone else. No one will ever come close to having my heart the way you have it."

My heart is imploding with pain. Why does he want me so much?

I don't understand why he loves me this much?

No one has ever loved me this hard or fought for me like this. No one has ever wanted me enough to give up their entire world just for me.

The idea of losing me agonizes him.

What does this mean?

I reach up and touch his face and his grip loosens. I trace my fingers over the perfect shape of his jaw. His eyes are glittering as though he is fighting tears. He is beautiful. In so many ways.

"Tuomo." I whisper his name, and he lets go, dropping his head onto my shoulder. "Everything is going to be ok." I say, stroking my hand over the back of his head, threading my fingers through his thick, dark hair. I've hurt him and my heart is breaking because of it.

He steps away from me and looks right into my eyes. His are dark brown pools of intense emotion. Looking right at him like this makes my heart go cold and the palms of my hands sweat. Fear replaces the heart ache. His jaw is tight, and his lips are pressed together. I no longer want to comfort him I want to run.

"You think everything will be ok?" he asks, but why does it sound like a threat instead of a question. Suddenly, my memory is back in my apartment, the very first time Tuomo showed up after all those years. When he pinned me to the bed, and I thought - I thought - I brush the memory away as my body becomes alive with lust because of it. No. Don't be ridiculous, Nerissa. Focus. Stay safe. Why do I keep confusing fear and desire?

He has that same anger in his tone, his body language, and his eyes.

"I - I think - we both just need time to think."

"Time to *think*?" he whispers with menace.

I force myself to take a slow breath in. I better think, quickly, if I want to get out of this situation. I glance left and right down the alley he has dragged me into. There isn't a person in sight.

"What are you looking for, little bird?"

Think, Nerissa, think.

"I was wondering if you have time to go for a coffee with me?"

He tilts his head to the side, narrowing his eyes. "Why?"

"Because this place is not the nicest - venue." I laugh light-heartedly, trying to change the mood. But my chest is tight with tension. "I don't want to stop talking to you. So, let's go for a coffee?" I shrug.

His shoulders drop, and he nods. "Alright. We can carry on talking." He holds out his hand and I swallow hard as I place my hand against his and he leads me from the alley out into the street. It's a lot quieter now, and above us the sky is dark. The streetlamps are shining pools of light and warmth spills from shop windows and small cafes along the walkway.

I feel so much better out here in the open, but I am well aware of the reality of the situation I'm in. Tuomo is a Vece. They do what they want - where they want. He could do anything he wanted to me right here in public and very few people would dare to interfere for fear of risking their own lives.

I point at a coffee shop just across the street and he pulls me towards it without a word.

We sit down and his eyes are burning into me.

The waitress comes and goes, and he has barely moved.

I wish there were more people in here. It's quiet. Not as reassuringly safe as I would have hoped.

When she brings our coffee and puts it in front of us, I try to ease the atmosphere by restarting the conversation. Tuomo is busy rolling the sleeves of his shirt up over his forearms, folding each roll, moving slowly, with strange purpose.

I clear my throat, hoping to get his attention.

"Tuomo, everything that has happened since you came back into my life has happened so fast. It's been really intense. I don't mean that its good or bad - but it's only been about three or four weeks and it's really confusing and overwhelming for me."

He stares at me, leaning back in his seat with his arms folded across his chest.

"So, because you got a little overwhelmed you want to throw what we have away?"

I shake my head. "No, it's not like that. I think we would both benefit from some space and time alone to just think about things."

He says nothing.

I try again.

"I need a week or two to clear my head so that I can sort everything else in my life out too. My job for example."

"A week or two." He voice is low and terrifying, the way he replies to me makes me tremble. But he is nodding. His body language and his tone do not match.

I've said enough. I need to stop talking now and let him process and reply instead of just repeating everything I am saying.

I pick up my coffee and sip it even though my stomach is churning, and I feel like I want to puke.

Tuomo takes his time. I feel like him watching me right now is some kind of power play, so I do my best to pretend that it isn't affecting me.

I still admire how gorgeous he is, even in the intensity of this moment. I can't help but notice how his forearms flex and the muscles ripple when he unfolded his arms to pick up his coffee.

He is quiet for a long time and my thoughts wonder about the safest way to get out of the strained situation I find myself in. I am halfway through my coffee when he speaks, and his voice has transformed.

"I think you're right." He sighs, leaning forward to pick up his coffee. "It has happened quick. And we both need to take a step back and reassess everything. I need to figure out what to do about my family and then we can talk again - take it slower."

Relief floods my heart.

"Yes, that sounds like the right thing to do." I sigh, relieved.

The rest of the conversation is strained and awkward.

We finish our coffee and stand to leave.

"Where did you park your car?" he asks, as we walk along the pavement.

"I walked here. It was a beautiful day."

"And you were going to walk home?" he says, vexed. "In the dark alone?"

"It wasn't that dark when I started walking home." I say. "I don't live far away at all."

At this point I think it is safer to gamble with the dark streets even in my neighborhood than it is to carry on spending time with Tuomo.

"I'll walk you home then." He says, and I can tell it isn't a question. Shit. I really wanted to get away from him. My thoughts are a muddle of confusion. One minute I feel as though being with him will only end in my death - and the next my body is craving him with feverish desire.

I need to get away from him.

"Thanks." I say, turning towards my apartment and walking in that direction with Tuomo walking close at my side. Smelling his body overpowering the other scents of the city and despite being afraid of him - I'm never safer than when I am by his side.

CHAPTER THIRTY-ONE
Tuomo

We walk along the dark streets in the cool night air. She stays close to my side. This area is notorious for being dangerous, and I could have gotten her a cab, or driven her in my car, but I want to slow down the last few moments I have with her for now. Her apartment is only a street or two away and while the area is dangerous, I am more dangerous. The people of this city, so matter whether they are high or low in social standing - they all know who I am and would not dare to mess with me. I am not afraid to walk here, even at night.

Nerissa is very alert and pressed against my side which is the reaction I was hoping for.

I can't believe she tried to break up with me. I felt carnal rage rip through me when we were standing in the alley way. I wanted to tear her to pieces at the thought of her rejecting me after everything I've done to make her see how much I love her.

If I cannot have her, no one can, and I was going to prove that to her right then and there.

But reason creeps into my mind even in the darkest moments and I know - she can push me away now - but soon she will be back and calling my name.

The fever of my anger faded when I reminded myself that she is going to find out she is carrying my baby in the next week or two. I have to be patient. I am so close to having her for good.

We walk in silence between each pool of light that forms a faded circle on the dirty road from the streetlamp ahead. It doesn't take us long to reach her apartment building.

I want to ask her if I can go in with her. Just for tonight. But I know she will say no, and it is far better for me to appear to be a gentleman at this point.

I've already slipped up tonight, letting her see the darkness in me.

It aches to think though - when I was at my lowest point tonight - she said my name and stroked my face and tames the beast in me with one touch.

How does she have that power over me?

Why doesn't she understand the potency of our love?

Is she denying it? Is she trying to pretend it's not there?

She turns towards me on the steps outside her building and smiles.

"Thank you for walking me home."

"Any time, little bird." My heart strains and stretches. How am I going to walk away from her tonight?

"I better go inside."

I nod.

I have to walk away. I will be back.

I wrap my hand around the back of her neck. "Take care of yourself. Call me if you need anything." I step close and kiss her on the lips. She hesitates for the briefest moment and then her hand runs up my chest. Fire burns across my skin as bolts of electricity shoot through me. The kiss lasts longer than I had intended.

I pull away, pretending to be the one in control.

"Good night, beautiful girl." I say, a heavy sadness creeping across my heart.

"Night." She whispers, stepping backwards, then turning away from me and hurrying up the stairs and into the building. Before she walks through the door, she glances over her shoulder. Her eyes lock with mine and I see the tears running down her cheeks.

Why won't she let me comfort her?

The door swings closed behind her and locks into place.

I turn my back on her building, shove my hands into my pockets and walk back towards where I parked my car.

Another week, or two - I can wait. Already my baby is growing inside her.

Instead of going home I head to a bar near my penthouse. I am too agitated to sleep. I need to bring my agitation down a few levels before I go home.

I order a whiskey, neat, on ice. Then I sit by the window overlooking the city and I sip it. Letting time drift forward, towards a future where her and I will be together without any of this annoyance. Without interruption.

It grows later and darker and finally, just past one in the morning, I am ready to go home.

Sleep doesn't come easily and when I wake up, my body is heavy and I'm angry the moment I open my eyes.

I thought, with how things were going between us, that I wouldn't have to use her pregnancy as a trap anymore. But thank fuck I had that back-up plan in place before any of this started. I thought things were going so well between us that if I asked her to marry me again, she would have said yes.

My brothers fucked it up by rushing into her apartment. Those assholes interfered where they shouldn't have.

But when I speak to my father in a few weeks with evidence that she is pregnant - he might hate her - but blood is blood, and he will never turn a Vece child away. He will have no choice but to accept her into our family.

What I need to do over the next week or two is focus on my work and try to ease the tension between my family and myself so that when the time comes to tell my father about the baby, he isn't full of hatred over what happened.

And I still want to watch her.

I have to.

It's in my blood and bones to be near her.

I will focus on my work. I will do my duties and every free moment I have I will be with her, near her and out of sight.

When I show up at the warehouse later that day to run through the shipment schedule and check up on stock levels my brothers eye me but say nothing other than hello.

It is awkward at first but when they see I am there to work and not cause any shit, they start to relax and get into the swing of things like old times.

My father doesn't show up that day, but I know Masaccio will report back to him. He always reports back to him. Like his little servant. His future heir. It makes me sick - the level of loyalty they have for that man.

After work I drive to her apartment and watch her from a distance. I have to make sure she can't stop me, I can't risk upsetting the appearance that I am giving her space as I promised.

She needs to think she is free of me for the time being.

Nerissa spends a lot of time on her laptop, job hunting, and she doesn't go out at all. I can already see the signs. I can already see the changes in her.

I wonder how long it will take her to notice what is happening to her body?

I watch and I wait and when I think about our future I smile.

CHAPTER THIRTY-TWO
Nerissa

I know he's there. Even when I can't see him, I can feel him.

Whatever connection we have is strong enough that it allows me to sense when he is watching.

I don't understand it, but I can't deny it.

It's been over a week since I asked him for time and it sounds crazy, but I'm finding his presence reassuring. I hate the fact that I want him close to me. I hate the fact that I'm relieved he didn't give up. He is being respectful in his own way by staying a distance away, but I'm glad he's still there.

I've been spending every waking moment looking for a job. I have been talking to the HR teams at the law firms I already applied to and trying to figure out why they keep turning me down. I even resent my application to a few of them to see if they would have the same response. It was the same. The same nonsense replies that make little sense.

At this point I am ready to march into one of their offices and demand to see a manager just because I need answers. How can I keep trying if I don't even know what I'm doing wrong? I need proper constructive criticism.

Places that turned me down have even hired a few of my friends from university, including Hayley, I did so much better at university than they did. It just *does not make sense,* and it's driving me crazy.

So, I can't get a job, and I can't stop thinking about Tuomo.

I can't get my life together and I am still in love with a man who is so many kinds of wrong for my life. It's hard to care that he might be wrong for my life when my heart keeps begging me to be with him. Maybe it wouldn't be that bad if I stopped fighting against what seems to be my destiny.

Tuomo is not giving up. Is that a sign for me?

I never did fully give myself to him. I always held back because of the fear of his family, his name and who he is. But he's never hurt me. He has protected me. He's kept me safe. And he's never given up on me.

Out of every person I have ever met in my life he is the one who would be there for me no matter what. Isn't that what every girl dreams of having?

I push my laptop closed and push it away from me, standing up off the highchair at my kitchen counter I stretch my arms above my head and yawn.

It's not even lunch time and I want to sleep again.

On top of everything else, I am exhausted.

It's as though the tiredness has crept into my bones.

I walk over to my bed and flop down onto it. My eyes are heavy and burning. I slept well last night, so I shouldn't want to sleep now in the middle of the day.

I brush it away, I am stressed. I have this constant worry weighting down on my shoulders and I am terrified that my entire future is falling apart.

Stress does crazy things to the body and steals your energy in the blink of an eye. They call it the silent killer.

I just need to rest, let my body take its time to realize that I am ok - I'm not in danger - and I *will* find a job.

Everything will be ok.

I remember standing in the alley way and telling Tuomo everything will be ok.

I can feel him right now, outside my window. Parked somewhere on my street with his eyes locked onto my window. He's there. I know he's there.

I fall asleep with thoughts of him drifting through my mind.

My body is rigid and aching when I wake up in the morning.

I thought a good night's rest would help - but now the stress and anxiety has turned to nausea.

I lie in bed for a moment, trying to ignore it. The bright light of morning is pushing into my apartment and making me squint against the white glare of my ceiling. I groan and close my eyes, but my stomach knots and tightens so I sit up. I hate being stressed.

The wave of nausea gets worse, and, in a flash, I am running for the bathroom.

I make it just in time. Throwing up everything I ate last night. I lean over the toilet gasping for breath. When I think it's over, I sit with my back against the cold tile wall with my eyes closed, breathing.

Dammit.

Everything is going wrong.

My eyes shoot open.

No. Fuck.

No.

It can't be - can it? I am on the pill. I can't get pregnant on the pill, can I?

I jump up and run to check my contraceptive medication.

I haven't missed any of them - but when I count backwards on the pills. I see I'm late. I was supposed to start a week and a half ago but with everything going on I didn't even realize. How in the world did I miss this?

Ok, but in all honesty, stress can make you throw up and be exhausted. I have seen people get violently ill from the stress of our final year at university.

I press my fingers against my tired eyes trying to push away the fresh worry that has crept into my mind. It's not working. The only way I can stop this panic is to do a pregnancy test.

I get dressed in a hurry. Not caring about showering or putting on make-up. Shoving my hair up into a messy bun I grab my keys and bolt out of the door to run down the road to the drug store.

Looking up and down the street while I make my way there - I don't spot him, but I can feel him.

I'm just being paranoid at this point. He's not here, Nerissa. Let it go.

I want him here, though.

If I'm pregnant, it's his baby and I don't want to find out alone.

The lady at the counter is so friendly. She can tell how worried I am, and she reassures me it's always a fright in the beginning, but no matter what the test results say it'll be ok.

Another person telling me it'll be ok.

Walking back to my apartment with the brown paper bag, gripping it in my fingers. I feel as though I am holding a giant red beacon - screaming the obvious to anyone who is watching - to him.

But I could have bought anything. Painkillers. Vitamins. I sigh and run up the stairs back into my apartment, slamming the door closed behind myself, I go straight into the bathroom to do the test.

There is no point in waiting - I couldn't even if I wanted to. I need to know right now.

Even though my bathroom is so small and cramped, I am still pacing up and down it. Moving from side to side, counting in my head. Counting again. Minute by minute. I don't dare peek at the test until the prescribed time is up. Because as soon as I see it, it's official. It's final and there is no going back.

I keep thinking to myself I must have mixed up the days or missed a pill somehow. Maybe I took it out of the sheet but didn't take it. My head has been such a mess it wouldn't surprise me.

The last-minute counts down in my mind and I freeze in place. I have to turn and look at it.

My eyes drift to the test and two very definite bright red lines on the small white window of the stick. I swallow. I breathe.

I wait for something to happen, but nothing does.

Reaching out I pick it up and stare at it some more.

I'm pregnant.

I have Tuomo's baby growing in my belly.

I am going to be the mother of a Vece baby.

Tears stream down my cheeks. On top of everything else this is frightening. It's a reality I didn't even consider was possible. I thought I had all the right precautions in place. I was responsible and careful - but not careful enough. This is a massive fuck up.

And all I want right now is to phone Tuomo. I want him here with me, right now, holding me. I want *him* to tell me that everything is going to be ok.

I need it to be ok. Nothing is ok.

I carry the test through to my bed and sit on the edge, still staring at the results.

What am I supposed to do now?

The thought of telling him about this is too much to handle. I have to think.

I have to tell him, right? He's going to be furious. I don't think he is the type of man who wants children. It will be a burden on his life - he's going to be livid with me and I'm terrified of dealing with that again.

I stand up, walking over to the window and staring out in the street below. Where is he? I can feel him. Does he know? Did he see what I bought? No, that's silly. He can't have seen. I need to tell him, he should know.

CHAPTER THIRTY-THREE
Tuomo

There has been a distinct change in her routine, and I know everything is falling into place. The last few days she has been sleeping in the afternoons and looking tired, even after the extra rest.

On top of that her skin is glowing, and she has a beautiful radiance about her.

The changes that are taking place in her body are small, just beginning, but I know her too well not to notice.

Of course, she is going through a lot and the stress of me not being at her side could make her tired too. But I'm certain there is more to it than that. This is more than stress.

She has hardly left the house over the past week - the last two days especially.

Excitement taunts me as I watch her.

I can't wait for her to realize what's happening. I'm curious about how she will react. Will she call me straight away?

It's early in the morning and over the past two days I am spending more and more time near her because it's going to happen soon, and I want to be there when she finds out she is carrying my baby.

She's still asleep up in her apartment and I am parked downstairs watching her window. I haven't been here long because I know her routine. I arrive just a few minutes before she gets up. This morning, she is sleeping later than normal.

The curtains are open as though she knows I'm here and is inviting me to stay.

I see movement in her home. She runs past the window towards the bathroom, clutching her stomach. I wait, a smile spreading wider across my face. The symptoms have become more obvious.

Not even five minutes later she is rushing out of the building, towards the drug store down the road and my heart is thumping with excitement. It's happening.

I get out of my car, staying on the other side of the street and a way back from her.

Nerissa looks worried. Her face is strained with a deep frown, and she keeps her head down as she walks. Her fists keep clenching and unclenching. I don't think she is even conscious of it. Her body is giving away her anxiety. She is panicking.

Inside the pharmacy I see her talking to the lady through the window. They chat for a while, Nerissa nodding at whatever she is being told. She pays for her items and then turns towards the swing doors and pushes them open. She glances up and down the street. I'm right here, little bird. I'm with you.

She comes out holding a brown paper bag which she is clutching as though it might kill her. Her fingers grip the paper, almost tearing it.

I want to grab her and hug her and remind her I love her. But I stay back. Hidden.

She hurries back upstairs, and I wait.

Two minutes.

Three minutes.

Five minutes.

She walks into the living room holding the pregnancy test.

She knows.

She disappears from view for a little while - then, to my surprise, she comes right up to the window, looking up and down the street as though she is searching for something. Or someone. *Me.*

It takes everything in my power to stop myself from calling her name.

There are tears in her eyes, and it breaks my heart that we couldn't have found out together. It doesn't matter though because soon we will be together, and nothing will ever pull us apart again.

Right now - I have to speak to my father. It's time to tell him that Nerissa is pregnant with my child, and he can no longer deny the fact that her and I belong together.

Reluctantly I start the car, needing to leave but not wanting to go.

"I'll be with you soon, little bird." I say, looking up at her window and the lost look in her eyes. It tugs at me, making me protective of her, aching to hold her.

But I have things I need to do. I have to make this right with my family. Then when she is ready to tell me about it, I will be ready to ask her to marry me again.

I pull away from her apartment building with a heavy heart, loaded with guilt that I am not with her in this moment.

I drive straight to my father's place. It will not be a calm conversation, because I know he's still furious and I am sure this news is going to make it worse before he processes the information but no matter what - I will tell him. And then I will marry her regardless of his reaction. With her being the mother of my child, he wouldn't dare harm her.

The mansion is quiet when I arrive. The loud, obnoxious noises of my brothers trampling through the place are not there. I walk into the front door and take a deep breath, my stomach churning, and knotting. It's cold and uninviting without my brothers here. At least they add some life to the empty halls.

"Tuomo. What are you doing here?" My father's voice booms through the house, coming towards me from down the hallway. I hear his footsteps approaching. He must have seen me on the security cameras.

"We need to speak." I say, pushing my shoulders back and standing taller.

He walks into the foyer, where only a short time ago I knocked him to the floor and showed him he was, in fact, not stronger than me. I wonder how today's conversation will go.

"Speak." He says, rough and cold. No greeting. No welcome. No fatherly love. There never has been, so it's no surprise.

"It's regarding Nerissa." I say and his face pulls tight, a sneer on his lips as he flexes his shoulder muscles. There is no point in dancing around the news so, I blurt it out right away.

"She is pregnant."

He stares at me for a moment, then shakes his head.

"It's not yours. Trash like that will be sleeping with everyone. What is she asking you for? Money? Is she blackmailing you? It might be easier to just give her what she wants to make this go away."

I roll my eyes, doing my best to stay calm because in this situation it's the only way to negotiate peace with him.

"I am one hundred percent certain the baby is mine. I have zero doubt in my mind."

"For fuck's sake." My father mutters. I can feel the disappointment oozing out of him. "So, we have a bastard fucking child carrying our bloodline." He sighs, running his fingers through his hair.

"Correct. But I will be asking her to marry me. My child won't be a bastard."

He nods. "She's a maid, it's a bastard." I want to hit him again, "we will have to fix this, so we don't look bad."

"She's a lawyer, not a maid." I remind him she is not her mother.

It's so strange how business like he suddenly becomes. With zero emotion he dishes out commands as though he is managing a meeting between board holders of his company.

"Contact the event organizer. We will have to spin this in the media as though it was planned. The wedding will need to be extravagant."

But I have no intention of letting him manage anything that is about to happen.

"The wedding is going to be private. An intimate affair without the media."

"Why do you have to make everything difficult for me, Tuomo?" He snarls. "*Fine*. Have your *intimate* wedding. But then I need an interview and an article with photographs of the two of you together for the press release."

He is negotiating as though this isn't about my entire future, and my wife, and my child. But negotiating is good none-the-less. It's better than flat out refusal to accept what is going to happen. Or worse, the reaction I expected, him having her killed.

"Fine. A press release will be acceptable."

Again, his cold eyes are piercing into me.

I stare back with as much intensity as he is delivering. This is *my life*. I will not give him control over it.

He looks away, then turns his back on me and walks off without another word.

I don't care. I have what I came for. I have my father's blessing. It would have been a hell of a lot harder without it - but I would have done it either way.

I walk out of the mansion lighter. Things could not be more perfect.

All I need now is for her to call me.

It's been seven years since I first saw her. I have been patient every single day, waiting for her, orchestrating our future and creating the events to place her in my path. And now I am going to be rewarded.

Since I reunited with her though, things have changed. My feelings have evolved into something new. If I know what love is - it's because of her.

CHAPTER THIRTY-FOUR
Nerissa

My phone shakes as I try to hold it still, but my hands are shaking so it's impossible. I've decided to tell him. What choice did I have, anyway? I always knew I would tell him. I just needed time to come to terms with my new reality before I faced his reaction.

I will do this with or without him.

I do not know how, because I'm broke and jobless, but I'll find a way.

Swiping my fingers across the screen I navigate to the messaging app and click on his name.

I struggle to type out the message.

> Me: Tuomo, can we please meet somewhere this afternoon? I need to tell you something. It is really important, and I would like to do it today if you are available.

My thumb hovers above the send button. Just press it. You have to.

I click send and the message double ticks.

He comes online and I drop my phone trying to lock it because I can't bear the tension while watching him typing out a reply that I have to wait to read.

Sitting on the edge of my bed with my eyes closed I wait for the tone of my messenger app. It doesn't take long at all. The soft vibration runs through me, and I take a deep breath.

His message is simple but friendly.

> Tuomo: Of course, I can meet you this afternoon. I'm free now if you want to meet at Red Roman on main street in about thirty minutes.

> Me: Yes. Thank you. I will be there in thirty minutes.

I was expecting to have time to think about what I wanted to say, but it's better to get this over and done with now. Sooner than later.

I nod to myself and gather my things, throwing my phone into my handbag. I decide to take the pregnancy test with me because I don't know if he is going to want proof. It's all the evidence I have.

Climbing into my old beat-up car, I haven't driven it for a while so I have to warm it up and let it run for a minute before I can drive it. It rattles to life with a choking sound. But once the engine has grumbled for a little while it sounds healthier.

I place my hand over my stomach, and for the first time, I feel a calm sense of connection to the little life growing in my stomach. I don't think I had really acknowledged it before, but as soon as I hold my stomach, protectively, tenderly I realize I am going to be a mother.

It's real.

I giggle, nervous amusement flushing through my cheeks.

"Let's go find out what your father has to say about all this."

I wish I was more confident as I walked into the restaurant. I wish I could just stride in here, smile and tell him the news and know - without a doubt - that no matter what his reaction is I can do this on my own.

But I need him. So, telling him today is not as easy as that. I don't just need his help financially, I need his support.

Is it wrong to need him?

Can I do this without him?

If I had a choice, I would choose him to be by my side.

I walk towards a table by the window. His back is to me as I approach but he turns around to smile at me before I reach him. It's as though he can sense when I am near as well. The same way that I sense him.

He stands up and wraps his hand around my waist, kissing my cheek. "It's good to see you, Nerissa." He is polite, friendly, void of the darkness I saw in him the last time we were together.

He pulls my chair out for me, and I sit down.

"Would you like a glass of wine?" he asks with a smile.

"No, thanks. A sparkling water will be fine for me."

"Are you sure?" he frowns. "They have the most amazing house wine here. I don't usually order the house wine, but this place —"

"Really. I'm fine, thanks. Just sparkling water."

He turns to the waitress who is standing alongside our table smiling, waiting.

"Two sparkling waters please and your starter platter."

When she's gone, he smiles at me and my heart somersaults. "I haven't eaten yet, and it's been a busy morning, so I hope you'll share a platter with me."

"Sure." I say, staring at him, falling into his eyes, picturing myself sinking into his gorgeous body. I sigh, squeezing my eyes shut. *Don't get distracted.*

He reaches across the table and takes my hand. His skin is warm against mine and it is all the reassurance I need. "What's wrong, Nerissa. You seem really stressed."

"The thing that I need to tell you - it's important that you understand that regardless of your reaction I will be - I will do this with or without you." I say, forcing confidence into my voice.

"Tell me." He says.

"I'm pregnant, Tuomo."

The instant I say it he is smiling. Not just smiling - he is *ecstatic*.

"Are you serious?" He asks, his voice overflowing with excitement.

"I'm serious." I say, a smile beginning to spread across my face too.

He stands up and drags me from my seat into his arms. His deep, genuine laughter rumbled against my body as it bubbles from his chest. He is kissing the top of my head and holding me so tight. I can't believe it. I can't believe how happy he is.

Suddenly I'm excited too.

He is *happy*. He isn't shouting or demanding I get rid of it. He's happy about this.

He lets me go and looks down at me. The dimples at the corners of his mouth are gorgeous. His eyes are bright and happy.

"I'm going to be a father?" he laughs.

"You are." I giggle. "I was worried. I thought - you would be upset."

"Are you kidding? This is the best news in the world."

He hugs me close again. "No wonder you didn't want wine." He chuckles. "I guess neither of us will be drinking for a few months, hey."

We sit down again, but Tuomo grabs the leg of my chair and pulls me right up against his. He holds me close to his side as he chats about finding the best doctors and asking me what I will need, then laughing and saying he'll start researching and make sure I have everything.

"I'll be there every step of the way." He says, brushing a strand of hair behind my ear. "You have made me so happy, little bird. And I don't want you to work until after the baby is born. If at all. I would prefer it if you just focused on being a mother. If that's what you want? It's what I want."

I lean into his shoulder, my heart is warm and happy. I don't have to do this alone. I don't have to worry about anything.

After our lunch I drive home, feeling like the weight of the world has been lifted off my shoulders. Tuomo has promised to take care of everything.

He is going to come over tomorrow so that we can discuss whatever it is we need to do.

I have a doctor's appointment in the morning, so I told him to come after that.

I sleep better than I have slept in a week, with no stress or worry on my mind.

At ten in the morning, I'm sitting in the doctor's office with a smile on my face.

"Here is a list of the vitamins I recommend you take." She hands me a piece of paper. "Did you have questions before you go?" She asks.

"Actually, yes." I scratch around inside my handbag and pull out the sheet of pills - my contraception. "I was on these." I hand them to her. "I wanted to know - because I fell pregnant while taking them does it pose any risk to the baby? Is there anything I need to do?"

She squints at the pills.

"What are these?" She asks, examining one pill.

"It's my contraception. The one you prescribed me months ago."

"No, honey. This looks very similar to your contraception but - look here." She pulls her drawer open and takes out a pill. She places it in my hand and then places one pill I was taking right next to it.

Almost identical. But not.

The contraceptive pills are smaller, whiter. My heart races.

"What are those?" I ask, a whisper.

"I think these are sugar tablets." She answers, frowning. "Where did you get them?"

I stare at her with my mouth hanging open. I don't know how to answer that.

She tilts her head to the side, looking worried for me. "Did someone have access to your contraception, Nerissa?"

"Yes." I answer, knowing that Tuomo has been coming and going as he pleases in my apartment -

whether or not I am home. "Yes, someone had access to it."

I leave the doctor's office shaking from head to toe.

I can't even drive.

The truth is too difficult to imagine. But I know.

I know he swapped the pills out and got me pregnant on purpose. He did this. He planned this. He tricked me. He bound me to him.

I sit inside my car, staring out of the front window at nothing. The world is spinning, and my vision is blurry.

What am I supposed to do with this knowledge?

I feel sick to my stomach.

I want to cry but I can't. I can't move. I can't do anything.

CHAPTER THIRTY-FIVE
Tuomo

She is late.

I'm waiting in my car outside her apartment, even though I know I could wait inside, I decide to be polite and wait to be invited.

But she's twenty minutes late. She should have been here already.

Getting more agitated and impatient by the minute I open the tracking app on my phone.

She's just arriving around the corner. Thank fuck.

I climb out of my car and walk towards the front door of her building. I watch her park, a smile on my face.

When she climbs out of the car I am standing right there, wrapping my arm around her and holding her for a moment. "Hello, little bird."

She nods, tense against me. "Hello."

"Are you ok, you're really pale."

"I'm having a terrible morning." She says.

"Let's get you inside. I read online that the morning sickness can be a lot worse on some mornings than others."

"Sure." She mumbles, walking as though she was in a trance.

I follow her upstairs and into her apartment.

She sits on the edge of the bed with a blank expression.

I pull the arm chair up close, pushing her knees apart I pull her into a hug. "It's going to be ok, little bird. We will get through this together. What can I get for you? Do you want some peppermint tea?"

"Sure." She responds, cold and distant.

What is going on? This seems too intense to just be morning sickness.

"Where were you now?"

"At the doctor's office."

I narrow my eyes towards her. "You should have told me. I would have gone with you. I want to be there for you at every appointment."

"Sure." She says again, pushing against my patience.

"Did the doctor say anything about the baby? Is it healthy? Are you healthy?" I ask with concern.

"We are both fine, Tuomo." Her voice is tight. Void of emotion.

I stand up, walking towards the kitchen to shake off some of the agitation that is building inside me. At the restaurant yesterday she was so eager - she was receptive and affectionate. Nothing like she is being right now. Pregnancy can create mood swings - but what is going on?

I make her a cup of tea and set it down on the bedside table. A powerful scent of peppermint fills the air. I close my eyes and breathe it in. When I open my eyes again, I feel a little more clear-headed. She is going to go through emotional highs and lows. I just have to be there for her. That's all.

I lean forward and take her hands. She doesn't look at me.

"Nerissa, we were talking a little yesterday about the future and I promised to take care of you. If you are worried about that - I don't want, you to be." I feel around in my pocket and pull out the velvet box.

A warm smile of excitement touches my face.

"I want to marry you. I want you to be my wife. I want to give you and our baby the entire world. I will spend every day trying to make you smile." I flip the lid open, revealing the ring I had made for her. The diamond bird. It has never belonged to anyone. It has no sordid history, no ties to my family's past. It is new and will only ever be hers.

"Will you marry me, little bird?"

Finally, she lifts her eyes towards me, but the anger in them makes me stagger backwards. I lean back in the armchair, my fingers clasping the velvet box. What is going on?

"Nerissa?" I stammer.

"I know what you did, Tuomo." She says.

"What I did?" I whisper.

She opens her hand and inside her clenched fist are her contraceptive pills. Well - not her pills - rather the ones I switched them with.

I swallow hard.

Fuck.

How did she find out?

I look into her eyes, meeting her gaze and holding steady.

"I know what you did." She repeats, her voice shaking at the edges. There is hatred in her eyes.

Or is it fear?

I can't tell.

I have never seen someone so upset. She is so full of rage that she is frighteningly calm. Like the eye of the storm.

"Nerissa."

"Don't bother telling me I'm mistaken."

I shake my head. "I wasn't going to. I admit what I did."

She looks shocked.

"Are you serious?" She shouts, suddenly breaking away from the calm and surging forward with fury. "You won't even try to tell me you didn't do it? Are you crazy? What you did is insane. It's such a devastating break of my trust - how could you do this and calmly admit it without even blinking an eye? You ruined my fucking life!"

She is shaking now - the storm is here. It's flooding from her eyes and her body in wave after wave of emotion.

I lean forward to hold her, but she shoves me away from herself.

"Don't you dare touch me." She growls.

"Nerissa, you need to understand why I did it."

"Oh - I'd love to hear this - go ahead. Tell me why you made this choice for me - go on."

I hold her gaze, staying steady, keeping my voice calm.

"Because I love you. And someone as incredible as you would never choose to be with someone like me unless you had a reason. I can't live without you.

You are my entire world. Everything good about me - is *you*. I am not even half the man I want to be without you at my side. I need you, Nerissa. I had to make sure I never lost you."

Her breathing hitches as she fights tears and her uncontrollable anger.

I reach out to her again, taking her hand. She doesn't move. I rub my thumb over the back of her hand, feeling the smooth warmth of her skin.

"Nerissa, please. I never wanted to hurt you. I did this so that you would let me love you. What I said before - I meant it. I will give you everything. I will give you the world. Can't you see I did this out of love?"

She's deathly silent.

"Please, talk to me." I beg her.

"I don't know what to say."

"Say you will marry me."

"Your family hates me. You lied to me. Got me pregnant, ruined the plans I had for my life. How can you ask me to marry you now? Have you lost your fucking mind?"

"No, little bird. I spoke to my father. I have his blessing." She glares at me, "There is nothing stopping us from being together. You will be welcomed into my family and our child will have the best of everything."

She brushes the back of her hand across her cheek to wipe away a tear.

"Please leave, Tuomo. Please just get the fuck out."

"No." I snap. "I won't let you kick me out of your life when I have fought so hard to be here. I won't leave until you understand how much I love you."

"But I need you to go." She says between tears.

I wrap my hand around her face. "Please, my love. Let me be with you."

She shakes her head, and my heart sinks to the churning pit of my stomach.

What have I done?

I've ruined everything.

I am always the disappointment.

My father was right about me all along.

I never deserved someone like her. I never deserved to be happy.

And she doesn't deserve to be trapped in a life with a monster like me.

I take the ring I had made especially for her, and I slip it onto her finger.

She stares at it. I wait a long moment, but her silence is breaking me. I can't take much more of this.

"This is yours regardless of your choice. It was made for you. It belongs to you."

She looks up at me.

The pain I see in her eyes is like a blade piercing my heart.

What if I have lost her forever?

CHAPTER THIRTY-SIX
Nerissa

Tuomo is staring at me and my heart is cracking and breaking to small pieces. I feel as though I will never be ok again. I am falling apart right in front of his eyes. The pain in my chest is agony that I never thought I would ever have to experience.

Just when I allowed myself to love him. Just when I was excited for our future together - I can't believe he has done this.

I want nothing more than to love this man. I want to give my heart and soul to him, but what I found out today has shocked me to my core. It isn't ok. It isn't normal to do this to someone.

I don't know what to do.

He holds my hand in his and pushes the diamond ring onto my finger. I stare at it.

It's gorgeous. I have seen nothing like it. The unique design tugs at my heart because it is obvious he has put a lot of thought into making this ring. He has been waiting for when he could slip it onto my finger as he has just done.

But I am sure that this is not how he imagined it happening.

"This is yours regardless of your choice. It was made for you. It belongs to you."

The weight of it on my finger and it feels right. It was made for me.

It has never and will never belong to another person because it was always meant to be mine.

Was Tuomo always meant to be mine?

Was he so sure of our future together that he was confident when he took the steps, he took to force us together?

How am I supposed to feel about this?

"Nerissa, I will be on the beach on Saturday morning at ten o'clock. I want to marry you. I will arrange everything, and I will be waiting for you on the sand, right at the water's edge. I will wait my entire life for you. Please, change your mind. Be there on Saturday. Let me love you."

I don't know what to say. Even if I had something to say my throat is closed so tightly over any words it would be impossible for them to be heard.

The hot tears spilling from my eyes.

Tuomo waits a moment longer, then he stands.

I am torn.

Torn between knowing I have to watch him walk away and running back into his arms and never letting him go.

I am so torn that I can't move.

He sighs, then walks out of my apartment. I don't look up, I don't watch him leave because I can't handle the pain in my heart.

What am I supposed to do?

Of all the people in all the world - why did I fall in love with *him*? A man so dangerous that he is willing to play games with my life like this. He would manipulate my future so that I had no choice but to be with him.

But I do have a choice.

My heart and my mind are at war.

I am in anguish.

The turmoil is crashing through me like a tornado.

I curl up on my bed, pulling my knees up to my chest and I cry harder than I have ever cried in my life. When I lost my mother, I at least understood what was happening. Humans understand death. It is a pain that we can embrace because it is a natural part of life.

This is a pain I don't understand.

It is an ache so deep and terrifying that I am afraid it will tear me apart.

I clutch my stomach, holding onto my baby, begging the universe to make things different.

Tuomo has shattered me.

I don't move from my bed until darkness creeps into my room.

It's been hours since Tuomo left and I've just been lying there, thinking, trying to figure out how this happened and what I am supposed to do about it.

I have one instinct that seems to take over.

The instinct to take care of my baby.

For the time being I can forget about how much I love that man, and I can focus on the very basic steps I need to take to keep my baby healthy.

One of those things is a healthy dinner.

Even though the thought of food horrifies me, I will make something, I will take my time, and I will eat it so that my baby can grow up healthy and strong.

In the kitchen I place the fresh carrots onto the cutting board and slice them into chunks. The beautiful diamond ring glitters each time I move my hand.

My eye is drawn to it.

My mind drifts back to every moment I have spent with Tuomo.

Each time he did something special for me, and each time I feared his intense love.

When he was, I leaned towards him, and when he was angry, I winced away. But the one thing that never wavered, despite the changes in him - was his love for me.

His anger was only ever a reflection of his fear of losing me.

His gentleness was the moments when he thought he had me.

Through everything that has happened - he has always loved me.

But it terrifies me he will do horrific things with the love he has for me. What else is he capable of?

I believe him though.

When he tells me, he will wait forever.

Because he has already waited years for me. I understand that now. Seven years, every day, he has been waiting for me.

I don't know what to do.

This decision that I have to make is going to affect my future in every way - and the future of my baby.

On Thursday morning a package arrives at my apartment.

It's a massive white box with a silver ribbon around it.

I carry it up to my room, placing it on the bed I stare at it for ages before I find the courage to open it. Because I know it's from him, and I don't want to be thrown back into that turmoil of needing to make a choice.

I'm a little nervous to know what he is giving me.

I tug at the silver ribbon, and it un-threads, slipping away from the box. An envelope falls loose, drifting off my bed and onto the floor.

I bend down and scoop it up. Sitting back on the bed with my legs crossed I pry the envelope open and unfold the crisp thick paper inside.

It is a letter from Tuomo, handwritten. I recognize his messy boy-handwriting, and it makes me smile. My heart clenches tight in my chest.

Little bird,

Please forgive me. I know what I did was unfair. It was wrong. I know it in the very fiber of my being, yet I can't say that I regret it because it has tied to me to you forever.

Please, come to the beach. Marry me. Let me spend the rest of my life showing you I am not the person I seem to be. I love you. I will show you that every single day in every way possible.

Forgive me, little bird.

Yours for eternity.
Tuomo
X

I blink back the salty burn of tears and clear my throat to sooth away the lump forming there.

Then I pull the lid of the box open and gasp.

Tissue paper falls away and reveals a wedding dress.

I lift it from the box and stand next to my bed, holding it out in front of me to take in the fine details and soft lace.

It is magnificent. Fit for a princess.

Standing in front of my closet mirror I hold it up against my body.

It's perfect.

I just wish everything else was perfect too.

Then this dress wouldn't be so heart breaking.

I hang the dress up on the side of my cupboard, but I find it too difficult to look at, so I carry it into the bathroom and hang it up on the back of the bathroom door. Even though it is out of sight I still can't stop thinking about it though.

It's like a flashing red light, demanding my attention, a silent alarm blaring in my mind.

What am I going to do?

CHAPTER THIRTY-SEVEN
Tuomo

The courier leaves my penthouse with the wedding dress wrapped in a thick silver ribbon.

It is no longer up to me to force her decision. I've done things that are unforgivable. I've taken a choice from her, purposefully putting her in a position that she never had a chance to think about or decide on.

What I did to her was evil.

I know that now.

I saw the look in her eyes, and it breaks me every single time I think it.

Closing the door behind the courier I walk back into my penthouse and sit down on the sofa, picking up the glass of whiskey I've poured for myself I take a sip. Then remember that I told Nerissa neither of us would drink during her pregnancy. It seems fair. Why should she have to give things up alone?

I put the drink back down again. My heart is heavy, and I want to numb the pain, but I can't. This is something that needs to be faced, accepted and acknowledged in its fullest. Because I am the one who did this. I am the one who created this situation hurting both of us.

It's Thursday. Two days until the wedding and two days until I find out if she will forgive me or not. I tried to keep the letter I wrote her short, but honest. Not wanting to drag out my side of things, but needing her to understand how deeply sorry I am.

Nerissa must be wanting to feel numb too. She must be struggling, alone, tired, emotional and drained from the pregnancy and the horror that I put her through.

She doesn't even know I stopped her from getting a job. I've already retracted all the requests I made at all the attorneys. Should she want to apply there again they would accept her in a heartbeat? I imagine that a few of them will send her an email offering her a job. I was told she is the top candidate in many of the law firms.

I don't want her to need to work - but if she *wants* to work - then I won't take that choice away from her. I'm done taking her choices away.

Picking up my phone I check my messages from my brothers.

They have all received an invitation to the wedding. My father received one too, but he won't be there - and I'm happier with it that way. But it would mean the world to me if my brothers attended.

Dalila is going to be there. She's been helping me plan everything.

Honestly, I've never seen her this excited for me. Her happiness and high spirits have been keeping me going these past few days. She seems convinced that Nerissa will be there.

I, on the other hand, am not. But I am hopeful.

Masaccio has confirmed. He will be attending the wedding with his wife, Leora.

A message from Celso comes through while I'm reading Masaccio's message.

> Masaccio: I will be there. I am happy that you found a resolution that no longer upsets the balance of our family. I wish you the best and I'm looking forward to celebrating the moment with you. Don't worry. She will show up.

He's always so serious. Not even an emoji, or anything that shows how he feels. It's a massive turnaround from the last time he spoke to Nerissa, threatening her to stay away from my family and forget about me. I need to leave all of that in the past and not hold it against him - in the same way that I hope Nerissa can forgive what I have done to her.

Celso's message is enthusiastic, and it brings a smile to my face because his support is letting me know that my family cares for me.

> Celso: Hells yes. I wouldn't miss it for the world. It'll be a tense moment, but it will end well when she walks onto the beach to marry you. I will be there for you brother, no matter which way it goes. I have tequila just in case.

Celso really proved himself to me when he helped me out of that holding cell. I have a newfound respect for him. He took a massive risk doing that. I will never forget it.

This journey I've taken with Nerissa has changed not only my relationship with her but also with my family.

My father, while still a raging asshole, has respect for me.

Masaccio and Rufino, I now understand why they handle father the way they do. I always thought they were sucking up - but - like me, they were just trying to survive his relentless attempts to control every aspect of their lives.

Dalila has always been there for me, and now is no different.

The most important thing I understand - is love.

Love cannot be forced. It cannot be bought. It cannot be faked or demanded or manipulated from someone. Love is raw. It's about sacrifice and giving - not taking. You cannot take love.

Love is accepting that no matter what you feel for someone - it is their choice, and their choice alone whether they will allow you to love them up close.

If Nerissa chooses not to be with me - then I will be forced to love her from a distance for all eternity.

And that teaches me something else.

That love is the most painful emotion of all.

I pick up my whisky and carry it to the kitchen sink. Pouring it into the drain I watch the gold liquid splash out of sight while the ice blocks spin and dance against the basin.

"Please, forgive me." I whisper to the air.

The heaviness in my heart is terrifying. Knowing that it will only get worse if she doesn't come on Saturday is even worse. How will I survive without her? I don't see a way forward without her by my side. My entire life is designed around being allowed to love her.

I turn away from the sink and head to the bathroom. It's late.

Tomorrow, Dalila and I are going to okay the last few aspects of the alter design and choose the flowers for the arch way that will stand on the beach. I need to be up early. I am exhausted, emotionally drained and tormented and overwhelmed.

A hot shower will ease my shoulders from the tension locked inside them and help me fall asleep easier.

I think of her every waking moment, so it is no surprise I dream of her every night. As soon as I close my eyes images of her gorgeous smile, her soft, caring eyes, those beautiful lips, and the way her hair flow like a river over her shoulders - she fills my mind and refuses to let me go.

I know she loves me. That is not in question. I just don't know if she loves me enough to forgive what I've done.

Saturday morning, nine forty-seven.

I am ready. I've always been ready - but right now I am standing at the altar, with my bare feet in the warm white sand. I am waiting for her. The black suit I'm wearing is crisp and well fitted. An archway curving over the alter is dripping with white roses and arum lilies. The ocean is turquoise and calm, and there isn't even a breath of wind. It's a perfect day.

Everything is perfect. The only thing missing is her.

Every time I glance at my watch it's only been one minute since the last time I looked, even though I'm sure it's been an hour..

Masaccio, and then rest of my family are here, sitting on chairs lined up on either side of a white carpet.

A haunting silence fills the space, leaving us speechless. There is nothing else to be said. All we can do is wait, and the waiting is killing me.

I look at my watch again and curse myself.

It's been thirty seconds since I last looked.

Taking a deep breath, I cast my eyes towards the ocean, because all I've been doing is staring from the fucking watch to the edge of the beach where she would arrive.

I'm going crazy. I will be nothing without her.

All I want is my little family. My perfect wife, my little baby, and all the love in the world. I want to create a home like I never had. A place filled with warmth and love and compassion.

It's all up to Nerissa.

My future is in her hands.

I can only hope that our love is stronger than the evil things I've done to her. I can only hope that she senses my love and finds it in her heart to forgive me.

CHAPTER THIRTY-EIGHT
Nerissa

On Saturday morning I wake up before the sun.

The quiet darkness of morning, just before dawn, is my favorite time of day. I've been missing it because I've been so tired. But my body woke me up this morning and now I am alert and rested.

But I still haven't made my choice.

I haven't looked at the dress again, I haven't even checked my phone.

I have no idea what I am going to do.

Quietly, alone with my thoughts I make a cup of tea and think about everything that's happened.

My most important question is - now that I am going to be a mother - how does it change what I want from life?

I know the answer, but I keep asking anyway, just in case.

I sit at my window sipping my tea with my eyes on the sky, waiting for the warm glow of sunrise.

I don't feel him here. I haven't felt him around for three days now. Since the dress was delivered. The dress that is hanging on the back of the bathroom door.

It's so quiet and peaceful.

My heart might even already know.

I haven't taken off the ring. It's still sparkling on my finger and catching my eye.

A ray of sunlight pierces through soft gray morning sky.

The smile that spreads across my lips is genuine and it fills me with happiness. I set my empty teacup down on my bedside table.

Picking up my phone I message Hayley.

> Me: I don't care what you are doing right now - I am calling a friend emergency, and I need you to come over right now.

If I am going to get married today. I want my best friend there with me.

And that means that I need to tell her everything - including the fact that I'm pregnant which I haven't shared with anyone yet.

I've been so alone these past few days, and I don't need to. I am surrounded by love. Some of it crazy, stupid, wild love - but it's still love.

I will give him a chance.

Because my heart wants to. All the fear I've had, has been the fear of losing him and regretting it for the rest of my life. I don't want regrets. All I want is him.

Hayley arrives in an array of worry and chaos, demanding to know what is going on.

I explain everything - then I have to explain again because it sounds unreal.

Through her disbelief and shock - she gets to a point where she grabs me in the tightest hug and screams in delight.

"I'm going to be an aunt."

"Well, you are going to be an aunt - but right now I need you to be a make-up artist and hairdresser."

"You're lucky I'm so good at this. Because if it was left to you, I doubt you would've even bothered to put mascara on." She laughs, grabbing her make up case out of her handbag.

We park at the beach at five minutes past ten and I am acutely aware of the fact that I'm late.

Will he still be there?

That's stupid. Of course, he will.

Hayley tugs my rickety door open, she was driving because there was no way I could get into the driver's seat with so many layers around my legs. She holds her hand out to me and lifts me from the seat, careful not to dirty or damage the dress.

"Wow." She says for the hundredth time.

"There's no time, we've got to go." I push her forward, slamming the car door behind myself.

Lifting the front of the dress I run barefoot onto the white sand.

He's going to be there. Just over this dune. Right at the edge of the water.

My heart is beating so fast I'm dizzy with excitement. I can't believe this is happening.

We're going to be married. I will be a wife.

"I see them." Hayley says, as relieved as I am.

And then I see them too.

Tuomo is looking right at me as I step onto the top of the sand dune.

My heart explodes in my chest, like one hundred fireworks all set off at once.

I walk down the dune, onto a white carpet that leads to him.

He looks incredible.

Adrenaline floods me as I walk past his brothers and his sister. I can't stop smiling.

My decision was so much easier than I thought it would be.

I always knew I was going to marry him, I was just fighting against my logic. But I love him far too much to let him go.

"Little bird." His voice is low, his eyes on me I feel as though I could lose myself in his stare.

"Tuomo." I whisper, standing beneath a high arch way of white flowers.

We stare at each, and the priest speaks.

I feel as though I'm in a dream.

Tuomo reaches out and takes my hand, his touch sending sparks through my entire body.

The priest tells a story of love, lost and found, and destinies that are intertwined.

The universe chose for us to be together. It was always going to end this way.

Even though this ending is only just the beginning.

"I now pronounce you husband and wife, you may kiss your bride."

Tuomo doesn't waste a moment. He steps forward, wraps me in his arms and kisses me. I forget the rest of the world exists.

Melting against him all I feel is the blissful pleasure of being in his arms.

He leans back, grinning down at me, the love in his eyes is making his face glow in a way I've never seen before. "I can't even describe to you how happy I am, little bird." He whispers against my cheek.

"I'm sorry I made you wait." I whisper back.

He shakes his head. "No, I am sorry, for everything. There are so many promises to make to you, but for now - all you need to know is that I love you more than life itself."

He kisses me again and his brothers taunt him, telling him to get a room.

Tuomo chuckles, his lips still pressed against mine.

He takes my hand, and we walk back down the white carpet towards a limousine, waiting just for us while everyone throws white petals around us. Tuomo holds the door open, and I climb inside.

"Where are we going?" I ask.

"On an adventure." He says, pulling me right up against his side.

The driver takes us all the way to the airport where a private jet is waiting for us. Tuomo lifts me in his arms and carries me onto the plane.

We strap in for take-off, but as soon as we are in the air he unclips me and lifts me to my feet again.

He carries me into what looks like a honeymoon's suite of an expensive hotel.

He grins and sets me down on the ground to take in the exquisite surroundings.

Stepping close to me he brushes his hand across my cheek, and I lean my face into his touch.

"I've missed you." He says, low and husky.

I stand up on my tiptoes and kiss him, with my hands around the back of his neck I pull him against my mouth. I want to taste him. I want every inch of his body against mine.

His hands run down my back, unzipping my wedding dress. He slides the straps off my shoulders and the heavy fabric falls to the floor around my feet.

"I didn't choose this." He says with shock, discovering that I am wearing white lace lingerie beneath it.

"You are not the only one who knows how to surprise the person they love." I grin.

A low growl rumbles through his chest as he pushes me onto the bed and begin tugging off his own clothes as he stands there admiring me.

I bite my lip, I'm impatient.

He kneels on the edge of the bed and grabs my ankles, tugging me closer to him. I giggle with excitement, and he glares at me with heat in his eyes.

"Spread your legs. Wide." He commands.

I do as he says, and he drops low, pushing his face between my thighs he grabs the white lace of my underwear and rips it from my body. Then he licks his warm wet tongue over my pussy.

I gasp, tilting my head back and arching my hips up towards him.

My body is burning with feverish need. Knotting my fingers in his hair I push his face against my pussy, rocking myself over his mouth.

He groans with pleasure his hands locked over my thighs, pulling them wider apart as I ride his face until I come with his tongue deep inside me, my lips screaming his name.

He sits up, crawling over me and pinning me against the bed with his body.

"You've had your pleasure, little bird. Now it is my turn." He growls, shoving my legs wide and forcing them open with his hips. He grabs my wrists and pins them above my head with one hand as his other hand explores my body, tearing the lace from my skin as he goes.

His cock is rock hard, pressed up against my pussy.

"I want you to fuck me." I plead.

"It's not about what you want anymore. It's about what I want." He chuckles with dark mischief.

"Please." I beg him again, lifting my hips, rubbing myself against his cock.

He pushes my hips back down against the bed.

His eyes darken and the smile that touches his lips makes me shiver with pleasure.

He thrusts his cock inside me, slamming himself deep into my pussy. I scream as he fills me up and spreads me open.

Then he slides out and does it again.

The pleasure is making me dizzy and wild with need.

He locks his hand over my mouth, using his body to hold me down he fucks me harder than he has ever fucked me before. His cock is pounding into me and my pussy is only begging for more of him, each time he buries himself in me I feel like I am going to explode, but then he pulls out and I'm desperate to have him back.

Tuomo uses my body for his own pleasure, but he knows what he's doing. He knows how to play me as though I was an instrument, and he was the artist.

He pushes me to the edge of coming, then drags me back and makes me wait while he builds the tension all over again.

Soon, though, I can't take it anymore.

My entire body is shaking when he leans close to my ear and whispers, "It's almost time, little bird." His words are like fuel on my fire.

His cock penetrates deep inside me and my pussy locks over him.

Wave after wave of pleasure pulse through me and he moans, deep and loud as he explodes inside me at the same time.

Tuomo releases his grip on my wrists, and I tickle my fingertips over his back.

He is still inside me, lying on top of me as we both breathe heavily.

He lifts his head to look into my eyes.

"In my wildest imagination, in all of my dreams, there could never be a more perfect wife. You are everything, little bird. You are my entire world."

About the Author

Hannah Rio is from a small town where she grew up reading romance books sent monthly by her book club. She developed a flair for crafting intricate love stories. She understands the delicate dance of heartbreak and joy. As a storyteller, she enjoys contemporary romances with strong, ambitious leading characters working through life's unexpected twists. Her female and male characters can make hearts flutter and eyes tear up. Her novels promise to bring readers back to continue events of new love and passion, secrets, surprises, painful memories, sassy and sweet, grumpy or good-hearted, and adventures with happy ever after endings.

Sign up to her newsletter here:

https://dl.bookfunnel.com/slno67x24w

- instagram.com/hannahrio2024
- amazon.com/author/hannahrio
- linkedin.com/in/hannah-rio-218707307

Also by Hannah Rio

BILLIONAIRES & BABY DADDY'S

Billionaire Baby Daddy Dilemma

Off-Limits Silver Fox Boss

MAFIA MEN

Vece Familia Series

Claiming His Mafia Princess

Something Old

Something New

Something Borrowed

Something Blue

Printed in Great Britain
by Amazon